HIDEOUS LOVE

—THE STORY OF THE GIRL WHO WROTE *FRANKENSTEIN*—

HIDEOUS LOVE

STEPHANIE HEMPHILL

BALZER + BRAY
An Imprint of HarperCollins*Publishers*

This book, although based on real events and real people, is
first and foremost a work of fiction. It consists largely of verse,
conversations, and descriptions that are fictional, although
attributed to real people as imagined or interpreted by the author.

Balzer + Bray is an imprint of HarperCollins Publishers.

Hideous Love: The Story of the Girl Who Wrote *Frankenstein*
Copyright © 2013 by Stephanie Hemphill

www.epicreads.com

Library of Congress Cataloging-in-Publication Data
Hemphill, Stephanie.
  Hideous love : the story of the girl who wrote Frankenstein /
Stephanie Hemphill. — First edition.
       pages   cm
  Summary: A free-verse novel about the Gothic novelist Mary
Shelley, a teenager whose love story led her to write one of the
great literary masterpieces, Frankenstein.
  ISBN 978-0-06-185331-9 (hardcover bdg.)
  1. Shelley, Mary Wollstonecraft, 1797-1851—Juvenile fiction.
2. Shelley, Percy Bysshe, 1792-1822—Juvenile fiction. [1. Novels
in verse. 2. Shelley, Mary Wollstonecraft, 1797-1851—Fiction.
3. Shelley, Percy Bysshe, 1792-1822—Fiction. 4. Love—Fiction.
5. Authorship—Fiction.] I. Title.
PZ7.5.H44Hi 2013   2013000237
[Fic]—dc23   CIP
                                                    AC

Typography by Ray Shappell
13 14 15 16 17 CG/RRDH 10 9 8 7 6 5 4 3 2 1

First Edition

For Jessica

I AM MARY

I want to be beauty,
but I am not.

I want to be free,
but I am not.

I want to be equal,
but I am not.

I want to be favorite,
but I am not.

I want to be loved,
and yet I am not.

MY MOTHER

I never knew my mother.
She did not nurse me from her breast.
She could not soothe my aches and tears.
I learned to walk without her aid.

I never knew my mother.
She did not hold me in the dark.
She could not sing away my fears.
I learned to speak without her voice.

I never knew my mother.
She helped establish women's rights.
I wear her legacy like a pledge.
I learned to think and fight reading her words.

I never knew my mother
for she died when I was eleven days old.

LONGING TO BE DADDY'S LITTLE GIRL

My father, William Godwin,
is a political philosopher
highly respected by his peers.
He is progressive,
teaching his daughters
as if they are sons.
When I stand in his presence
I feel as though I must
leap upon a chair
just to meet his shoulders.
My father, William Godwin,
is a tower of light.

MY STEPMOTHER

She was spawned from creature,
not man, and sends shivers
up one's arms.
Under her hair must be horns.
She is Medusa
trying to turn me to stone
in the eyes of my father.

At times I swear
she was born to torture me
and for no other purpose.
She needles me
with her incessant blather.
She prods me to misbehave
when she stupidly
misuses language
and forgets facts.
She picks on me
for my impatience with others
as she herself is small-minded.
She criticizes me for not being
as pretty as her daughter, Jane,
despises me for not being Jane.

She reflects no history,
nothing of which to be proud.
All she bears is the marital hand
of my father which baffles me
more than snow in July.

She shuffles me away
to Dundee, Scotland,
when I am fourteen
and for that I *am* grateful.

OUR UNUSUAL HOUSEHOLD
1814

Fanny is the eldest,
my half-sister, daughter of my mother
and Gilbert Imlay, an American enterpriser.
She never seeks trouble
and is quiet and reserved.
Her stated last name
is the same as my father's, Godwin.

Charles Clairmont, the next eldest,
is the son
of my awful stepmother,
Mary Jane Clairmont
and Charles de Gaulis,
who died when Charles was one.
Charles is fair haired,
and fortunate to be a boy.

I am the third eldest
and best bred.
Learning comes easily to me,
as does frustration.

Clara Jane Clairmont (Jane)
is nearly my age,
the daughter of my stepmother
and some unnamed suitor
my stepmother calls Charles Clairmont,
yet not the same man
as was Charles's father.
We sometimes get on
and at other times I wish
to pull Jane by the roots of her hair.

And then there is William,
the youngest,
the offspring of
my stepmother and my father,
doted on by my stepmother
until it pains the eyes.

None of us has the same parents.

MY RETURN FROM DUNDEE, SCOTLAND

Spring 1814

At first I was afraid
to leave my home,
to leave my father's care,
knowing that my banishment
to the Baxters
meant to punish me.
My arm of pustules and pain
represented all the ways
I could not be well and good
in my own house.

But I found a family in Scotland.
A family like I had read about in books
where the mother and father
care for one another
and all the children
are their own.

I found girl friends in Scotland,
the two daughters of the Baxters,
Isabella and Christina.
We became as inseparable
as words and letters.

My arm healed
and my temper soothed.
My imagination awoke
like a sleeping giant
in that stark landscape,
and I began to write stories.

I return to my house
of chaos, calmer
and more assured.
There is so much
of the greater world
I know now
will be a part of me,
and I am not afraid.

MR. SHELLEY
May 5, 1814

He is the buzz
of our Spinner Street home
when at sixteen
I return permanently from Dundee.
No other topic passes between anyone's lips.
Jane declares that when Mr. Shelley
falls silent
the air ceases circulation,
that when a smile flushes his countenance
the room boils with laughter.
And even quiet Fanny agrees.

But I remembered Mr. Shelley
from my visit home
the year before
as more buzzard than noteworthy,
fairylike
with the curly blond hair
of a schoolgirl,
his hands frail as silk stockings.
I remember he stood beside
his wife and I wondered
who wore the dress?

In a voice pert as a baby starling,
he had proclaimed my father was a genius
who deserved his financial support,
and I admired Mr. Shelley for that.
But the ceaseless obsession
that my stepmother, the woman of scales and dread,
my siblings, and even my father
seem to have for Mr. Shelley is comedy.
No man can live up to it.

Jane smirks, "You'll see,
his noble birth, his high ideals—
You'll choke on your coal-stained doubts."

I roll my eyes at my stepsister,
thump downstairs in my blue everyday frock,
because why would I dress up
to dine with some pansy of a man?
Even his name sounds like a girl, Shelley.

But when I slink
into the parlor
Mr. Percy Shelley
traps his gaze
upon my brow
so tight
I cannot inhale,
and then he gasps
as if I am a masterwork.

I stand stunned.
He genuflects before me.

No one has ever looked
at me, and certainly
no one has ever looked at me
like this,
like I am anything sigh-worthy,
something to hang diamonds on.

This man who owns
the breath of my father
stares at me
as though I am holy.

When Mr. Shelley
introduces himself to me
this second time,
I swear I smell rosehips
and lavender on his palms.
I glance around
and smile
to find that this evening
his wife is not in attendance.

WHAT IF HE LIKES ME?
May 1814

What if it was not only awe
and admiration for my breeding,
but something more that caught
Mr. Shelley's eye,
something particular about me?

What if he calls again,
what shall I wear,
how coy should I act,
what exactly have I to say to him?

What if he didn't care
for me at all and I imagined
the moment happening between us?
What if he never calls again
and I am left to wonder
what might have been?

He is yet a stranger to me,
and then somehow I feel
as though I have known him
for many years now,
as though he may be the one
I imagined would come
and whisk me away
like a valiant soldier
rescuing me from the prison
of my house.

HE COMES TO CALL
May 1814

At first one can
be certain whom
Mr. Shelley intends
to visit and that name
begins not with an *M*.

He and my father
argue into the night
about politics while
Jane and I hide on the stairs
catching phrases as if they sate,
like they are crumbs for the starving.
We listened to Mr. Coleridge's poem
The Rime of the Ancient Mariner
when I was a little girl
in much the same manner,
hiding behind a chair.
I saw nightmares because
of it for a year.
Now what I hear,
the sweet tones of Father's
and Mr. Shelley's sharp intellects,
breeds dreams when I sleep.

He glimpses me
one night as I linger
in the stairwell
and the next day
when Mr. Shelley calls
he requests me,
as well as Jane,
whose attendance I hope
is for nothing more
than to dissuade suspicion.

When Mr. Shelley and I meet
I will certainly stutter.
I will fall down the stairs
before I have a chance to speak.
I must remember that everything
I say reflects upon my brilliant parents.
For once I wish to bite my tongue.

LIKE MY FATHER
May 1814

Mr. Shelley does not dote
on Jane. She is but
furniture to him.

"You are finer
than your surroundings,"
he says to me.
"I see it in your
broad forehead—
intelligence, cleverness."

I blush until my cheeks
become the color of my hair.

He gestures to the portrait
of my mother above
the mantel. "I know
the writings of your mother;
have you read them?"

I nod my head.
I wish for words
to pour from my mouth,
as usual, but today
I stand mute.

"You too
have great things to write.
It is your lovely fate.
And I believe I will
be your guide."
His winsome eyes snare me.

And somehow
I feel in my heart
that he may be right.

WALKS IN THE PARK

June 1814

We see each other
on the forested grounds
of the Charterhouse school.
Jane and I pretend
to my stepmother
that we are just out for a walk,
but all my joy wraps
inside those moments
when Shelley
joins us and then asks
Jane to stand at a distance
for he and I must speak
of philosophical things.

"What is the purpose of poetry?"
Mr. Shelley asks me.

Today I do not hesitate to say
"To enlighten. To heighten
one's awareness of the world
and one's place therein.
Or some might say
to capture beauty at its
most vulnerable core."

"What is beauty?" he demands.

"An ideal." I smile.

"You jest, but nothing
is too ideal
that can be imagined."
He looks as though
he might grasp my hand,
but instead breaks off a branch.
"Poetry is political."
He swirls the branch at me
as if it were a sword.

I feign as though
I have been wounded.
"I know."

PAPER BOATS

Summer 1814

Jane and I watch
as Shelley folds the paper
into triangles.
He fans out the bottom
so his creation
resembles a little ship.

"All you need now
is a crew," I say.

He shakes his head.
"I require another vessel."
He quickly transforms
paper into boat
and hands me one.

"Shall we test their might?"
I ask him, cradling his gift.

"First we must christen them.
I hereby name thee the *Wollstonecraft*,
the strongest, most brazen ship on the sea."
And he gives his paper boat a shove
onto the river.

I thrust my craft forward,
"And I christen thee the *Shelley*,
the master of tides, the builder of ships."

Our paper boats crest
the river's pooling,
floating along the shore
together.

"Your construction
withstands the waters."

Shelley smiles and lights
a match. "But not fire."

He flames our cruising ships
so they are pyres
upon the water,
brilliant and smoking
upstream.

Jane and I clap our hands.

LOVE AFFAIR
Summer 1814

I shall wear my tartan
dresses now
for he is as dear to me
as the Scottish countryside
from whence the material came.

I am enraptured
in his high ideals
bound up in clouds
of his noble thoughts.

He stares at my crown
of red hair
and I swear he admires
not only the resemblance
I bear to my mother's portrait
over the mantelpiece,
but also the match of what
lies beneath.
He worships the best
part of me,
that which most men
would discount,
that which gives
me greatest pride,
my brain.

We talk of politics
and literature
and he vows
to be my new instructor.

He is generous
like none I have laid
eyes upon.
He gives his shoes
to the poor when he has no coin.

Like the monarch's
two wings
I can match
him wit for wit.
We fit glove to hand,
and he praises the finding
of an intellectual equal.

I am happier now
than ever I have been,
more joyous
than when I am reading
my favorite book.

IS THERE ONLY ME?

June 1814

My feelings overtake me
more swiftly than quicksand
and I tend to forget
that I alone do not grace
Mr. Shelley's life.

His wife, Harriet, came before me
when she was but my age
and Shelley unburdened
her from her life of confines
as he promises to do for me.

I may be many things,
but I wish never to be a fool.

AT MY MOTHER'S GRAVE
June 26, 1814

The stone reads
Mary Wollstonecraft Godwin.
I learned my alphabet
under the shade of this willow,
spelling out letter by letter
the name Mother.

Jane finally retreats
like a sad pup
and leaves Shelley and me alone.

Shelley grasps my hand.
"I have been on a long quest
for love. You are a dear friend
to me, but dearer more than that."
He pauses; his piercing blue eyes ignite.
"I was an unhappy boy at Eton,
bullied and misunderstood.
I have a father who thinks
me mad for my principles
and at times would have liked
to commit me to an asylum.
I have been tempted and obsessed
with magic, with chemical experiments,
and with death,
and shall likely always be.

"But all of this has made me
the man that I am—
one now devoted to you."

I feel light-headed
as though I
hang upside down.
I almost don't want to ask,
but I must know.
"What of your wife, Harriet?"

He tucks the hair
behind my ear and whispers,
"I am not sure that she
is so devoted to me anymore.
I can't even be certain
that the baby she carries is mine."
He sits up straight
and adjusts his collar.
"We are no longer married
in mind nor spirit,
nor love.
We never were a true match."
While these words
trickle from his lips
he looks deflated,
as if someone draws
blood from his face.

My mother wrote
about the constraints
of marriage and warned
against its conventions
and restrictions, for women especially.

This love I feel
for Shelley may come
but once,
and I wonder, Mother,
what to do?

I wrap my arms
around his wiry frame
and confess,
"I am completely yours."

JANE

Summer 1814

My stepsister plays a role
she seems to well like,
the conduit for the love
that Shelley and I have found.

She is a river
that brings Shelley and me together
by chaperoning our time.

Her generosity
might be perplexing
except that she
loves a good romance novel,
and in this affair
she is like the paper
upon which we
write our story.
She is necessary
to us right now,
and it seems
Jane loves little more
than to be needed.

FATHER FIGURE

July 6, 1814

Father is outraged.
The house quakes
with anger
as though we have
upset a hive
of frightened wasps.

Shelley asks my father today
to be with me
and a resounding "No!"
echoes through all chambers.

Father must have
forgotten his own
principles of free love
and his proclamations
about the absurdity of marriage.
He banishes Shelley
from ever seeing me
as Shelley is married to Harriet.

Always more God
than man,
today Mr. Godwin decides
to act as any ordinary
father.
I am perplexed.
Stepmother must be at root.

LAUDANUM

July 1814

Letters pass
as I am trapped in the tower
of our home and Shelley
is forbidden to see me.

Jane secures our secret notes,
our wily messenger pigeon,
while Fanny frets
that we will be found out.
My brothers, as usual, pay no mind
to anything not concerning them.

I miss the smell of Shelley,
the earthy, mad look in his eyes.
He sends me his book-length poem,
Queen Mab, inscribes the book to me,
renouncing Harriet again.
"Love is free,
to promise forever to love
the same woman is not less absurd
than to promise to believe
the same creed: such a vow,
in both cases, excludes us
from all enquiry."

Shelley finally cannot be held back.
He dashes into the schoolroom
of our Skinner Street home
with a wild look.
He holds out a bottle of laudanum
and brandishes a small pistol.
"Swallow this bottle," he pleads,
"and we shall be united in death."

The color drains from my face
as though my love shoots
a bullet into my heart.
Tears plunge down my cheeks.
"Please don't harm yourself.
Go home," I beg.
"I am eternally yours already.
I pledge you fidelity forever
if you will only see reason."

Shelley looks mystified
as though he may have ingested
the poison before arriving here.
Still he tucks the pistol
in his belt and, deflated,
ambles to the door.

He leaves the bottle of laudanum behind.

WITHOUT ME
July 1814

I hear that my love
takes an overdose
of laudanum,
and the doctor has been called.
I hold tight the bottle
Shelley left for me
and wonder if I should,
in some Shakespearean manner,
swallow its contents as well.

I learn Shelley will survive,
but Jane and I
are trapped,
not allowed
to breathe fresh air
as though we are
petty criminals.

Fanny tries to cheer me
with news of Shelley,
and the porter of our
little bookshop
exchanges letters for us,
but this will not suffice.

I must see his fragile face,
know for certain
that he will thrive.

Sleep is beyond me.
Food holds no luster.
One could drink my daily tears
by the teacup.

Father and Stepmother
know nothing of love,
know nothing of the pain
it feels to have one's limb
separated from one's body.

This will not do.

ESCAPE

July 24, 1814

Black bonnets strapped
to our chins,
silk traveling gowns
corseting our ribs,
Jane and I cat out
into the dark morning.
The air at four o'clock.
is wet with heat.
Our nerves charged
and excited as a murder
of crows after shotgun fire.

Shelley's velvet arm
dangles over the carriage door.
His left boot taps
impatient, impatient, impatient,
as a child
awaiting our arrival,
eager for our departure.

He settles Jane
like a delicate vase
carefully into her chaise.

I think I hear
boots on the cobblestone,
think I distinguish
the faraway echo
of my father's voice,
but it is only horse hooves.

With one hoist into that carriage,
my lover orphans me.
He cloaks me in the cushion
of his arms and we race
away from Spinner Street
on the bumpy road to Dover.

A BOAT TO CALAIS
July 1814

Weak from carriage travel,
I collapse, limp as wilted greens.
Shelley was certain
we would be pursued
and hired out four horses
to speed us along.
I have to breathe fresh air
and walk about
every time the carriage stops
to keep from vomiting.

We cross the channel
in a small fishing boat.
The water begins calm
as a sleeping dog
but then churns up
into a rage of storm.
Our little boat tosses
to and fro. We sit on the boat's hull,
my head upon Shelley's quaking lap.
He fears we will die
on this little raft.
Yet he is not sad,
for in death we will unite
never to be separated.

The storm quells
as we approach France.
Dawn breaks in streams
of orange and pink.
Shelley believes
this to be a good omen.
His spirits lift
like a fog dissipates.
"A bright future lies before us,"
he says.

A BRIGHT FUTURE
July 1814

I see my future
now not as something
intangible like a dream,
but like a boat
meeting land
after time spent at sea,
a destination I will reach.

Shelley holds my hand
when the water
splashes inside the boat
and the sky troubles
itself with a wicked storm.
He sings to the birds of the air,
charms even the wind
with his words.
He accompanies me,
a noble partner,
as I travel
toward my life.

RETRIEVING CLARA JANE
July 29, 1814

Our beyond sterling reputations
tarnish
by a single expedition
it seems.
The rumors abound
about our elopement.
Harriet, Shelley's wife,
goes so far as to say
that my father
sold me and Jane to Shelley
for fifteen hundred pounds.

Stepmother arrives in Calais
with the intent to return to London
with her daughter in tow.
I am beyond saving,
and besides, my father
did not come after me.

Stepmother sends a note bidding
Jane come see her.
Who knows what sorcery
and threats she employs,
but by night's end
she convinces her daughter
to accompany her back to London.

Jane wishes to see Shelley
one last time
and inform him of her plans.
Why must Jane have counsel
with Shelley alone, I wonder?

Within the hour
Jane decides to continue
on our European adventure
and leave behind her family.

My elopement with Shelley
seems to acquire an air
of permanence now.
And it seems that Jane
may well be entangled
in that arrangement.
But do we really need her
anymore?

I already share
Shelley with Harriet.
Must I also share him
with my stepsister?

NEVER ENOUGH MONEY

August 1814

We embark on
our European adventure,
a sense of daring
on the horizon.
Shelley and I begin
a joint journal of
our travels.
Jane, never wanting
to miss out on anything
we do, takes to her own pen
as well.

We carriage to Paris,
but dear Shelley
did not plan well enough
for this journey.
Sadly we haven't the funds
we need to continue
on to Switzerland directly
and in the same manner.

Paris is not the city
I expected.
The art lacks spirit
and the gardens stand
formal and dull
as ladies of the court.
But I elope with my dear love,
pursuing my heart and mind,
and break away from Stepmother
and Father
and all of their restrictions.

When we haven't a pound
in our purse,
Shelley asks his publisher
to forward him money.
But all he receives
is a cold rebuke.
I am not worried for
"*omnia vincit amor,*"
love conquers all.

My Shelley sells
his watch and chain
and after much fuss
obtains a loan
for sixty pounds.

Jane and I spend
hours trapped together
with nothing to do
but stare at our bonnets
and practice our French.
I question again
why she is even here.

Shelley says if we are prudent
we can travel
the two hundred fifty miles
by foot to Switzerland
and afford it.

Jane and Shelley
leave me alone
as I ail
and purchase a donkey
to carry our wares.
Halfway to the next village
it appears Jane made
a poor choice of animal;
the donkey buckles
like a woodsman chopped off its legs.
We trade the donkey
along with some money
for a mule. But then
my Shelley sprains his ankle
and must ride the mule.

It must be quite
an appearance
to see Jane and me trudge
behind in our silk traveling gowns,
the flies at a constant swirl
about our heads.

Road travel is dirty
as a beggar's shoe,
and the inns where we lodge
are inhospitable
to anything but rats.

Still, I have my Shelley
and my freedom
and that is all
I truly require.

FREEDOM

August 1814

Unfettered,
with a pen in my hand,
I am as a colt
released from her fence.
I rush toward
new scenery,
devour the landscape
because I have never
witnessed, unbridled,
such freedom before.

I wish to record
every detail,
do not want to forget
the breeze and smell
of each new land
we touch.

For perhaps if I find
the right words
Father will understand
why I left.

TRAVELING TO SWITZERLAND
August 1814

After much heat and dirt,
but little debate,
we abandon the idea
of walking to Switzerland
and trade the mule
in part for a carriage.
So we travel once again
as we began.

Shelley in a whirl of excitement
like one struck by electricity
loses touch with the ground
on which he stands.
I shock to discover that
he writes to Harriet
and invites
her to join us on this journey,
as a friend.
Of course
she would have to travel alone
to meet us and
is five months pregnant.
He asks her to bring
some legal documents.
That Shelley's letter to her
receives no response
does not surprise me.

The majestic Alps
embrace me like a father.
I gasp in their presence
and will never forget
the power they wield
just by existing.

The Swiss are as clean
and welcoming as the French
were not. Our carriage driver
says it is because they have
no king to fear.

Shelley finds
a friendly banker,
but the bag of coins
he returns with still cannot
completely fund our expedition.

We rent a house
on a six-month lease
at Brunnen, but the old-fashioned
stove that heats
the two rooms nearly suffocates us
when it functions.

Shelley tells me
as we read Tacitus
that our sixty pounds
have dwindled to thirty.
We possess just enough money
to return home to England
if we travel up the Rhine
through Holland.

Jane reads *King Lear*
and on the first stop
of our journey home,
leaps into the bed
with us as she sees
night visions of the dead.
I call them Jane's horrors.
Shelley of course consoles her,
and I swear I catch Jane
wink at me
like she plays the fox
outwitting the hound.
I will trap all eyes
upon her now.

I grow weary of this travel
as a threesome.
And I often fall ill
for some reason.

But my lover holds me dear
on my seventeenth birthday
and reads to me
from my mother's book.
I soon forget my woes.

THE TROUBLE WITH JANE
August 1814

At first I believed
that Jane accompanied
us just to escape
the tyranny of the household.
I thought that she longed to see
the world, expand her mind,
and be liberated from
the society into which we
were so assuredly to enter
and, as women, be forced
into the roles of wife and mother.

Her design may have been
larger than that.
I notice when she eyes
Shelley as though she might
lick his glove.
I do not believe I have ever
wanted to throw
anyone out of a carriage more.

Perhaps we should have
brought my sister Fanny
along instead.

HOMEWARD BOUND
September 1814

Shelley and I religiously record
our journal
of European travel.
We voyage far enough
to see Lake Lucerne
where my father's book
Fleetwood was set.
Father looked to escape
materialism in his book,
but unfortunately we find
it too expensive to remain.

We continue our practice
of daily reading and writing.
Lord Byron's *Childe Harold's Pilgrimage*
fills us with the same delight
as does a vivid painting.
Shelley writes his novel *The Assassins*
and I compose my story "Hate,"
while Jane works on "The Ideot."

When we arrive in
Rotterdam all our money
has been spent.
Shelley persuades the captain
to return us to England
on the condition
that he will be paid
once we arrive.

We have traveled forty-two days
and slept in forty-one different locales.

We reach England
by morning's cry
nearly drowned
by the storm's brutal winds,
tossed about like seaweed
on the waves.

When we approach London,
we row up the Thames
in a little boat
while Shelley desperately
attempts to find funds
to pay the captain
for our crossing.

Finally he stops
on Chapel Street
at Harriet's father's door.
He emerges
not with his wife
but with finance.

He says, "I told Harriet that
I am united to another.
And that she is no longer my wife."
He clutches my hand and says,
"I spoke of your courage
and told her you had resigned
all for me."

And my love is correct.

MY LOVE
September 1814

My love nurtures me
like rain
cultivates a field.

My love astonishes me
like light
amazes a moth.

My love enlightens me
like language
imparts meaning.

My love changes me
like time
transforms a mountain.

My love strengthens me
like a double stitch
reinforces a seam.

My love perfects me
like diligence
rewards its student.

RETURN TO ENGLAND
September 1814

I did not expect
open arms, I suppose.
But when I live
according to my father's
philosophy of love and friendship,
his idea that it ought be measured singly
by what we know of its worth,
and he refuses to see me,
worse, disallows
my sister and brothers
any contact with me,
I see his patriarchy
somewhat as an attack
on the principles
set forth by my mother.

I cry into my pillow
like I did when I was a child,
sob myself to sleep.
I cannot make sense
of his rejection
of me when I choose
to live my life
in the exact manner
he has written
that one should live.

Father expects
Shelley to support him
financially, as the rich man
should help his poor brethren.
Harriet requires funds, as well,
and yet we starve, change
our lodgings nearly nightly.

I write to my dearest friend,
Isabella Baxter,
and I receive a cold letter
from her husband
who forbids her contact with me.

It appears that to live out
my parents' ideals
comes at heavy cost.
I am now as notorious
as was my mother
and therefore chastised.
No one comes to call
except for Thomas Love Peacock,
the poet and novelist
who advocates for Harriet,
and Thomas Hookham,
Shelley's publisher.

Jane nags at me
night and day,
a gnat about my neck.

I touch the small bump
below my waist.
There seems
to be no doubt
at this point
that I am pregnant.

My child will likely be born
while my Shelley
is married to another.

My fear swells
as does my belly.

SUNDAY
October 1814

I tire, sleepy
as an old cat.

Shelley's creditors
set the bailiffs
on him, and he can no longer
live with me and Jane.
He resides with Thomas Love Peacock
when he can, or at some
flea-infested hotel.
He tries like a gentleman
to arrange further loans
to pay off his debts,
but they often treat him
as a beggar.

He writes letters
to make me sick
with love for him
and lonelier than a bird
without wings.
He says he feels
in my absence degraded
to the level of the vulgar and impure.
I promise my enduring
love and that I will
never vex him.

We steal conversations
on the steps of St. Paul's,
but the only time I own
with my Shelley
is Sunday,
when the bailiffs
are not allowed to make arrests.
We spend all day in bed,
reading and talking,
scheming his next move.
Sundays I am alive.

SISTERLY LOVE
Autumn 1814

Jane skulks about the house
we can now sometimes share
while Shelley and I
stay in bed
and read and write together—
always
her pouty little complaints
like a child's smudge
on a pristine canvas.

I do not trouble
Shelley with my every ailment.
But Jane pesters Shelley
with her night traumas.
Her pillow mystically
moves from the bed to the chair.
She acts so terrified
that Shelley is forced to give up
his spot in bed
so that Jane might
have me as companion
while she sleeps.

Shelley loves to scare her
and it sometimes frightens
me how well they get on,
especially when I am too sick
to take a walk
and they gad about town
together
without me.

Jane has now adapted
her first name
and wants to be called
Claire Clairmont,
as she thinks
this makes her sound
more literary.

I fear my stepsister
is not very sisterly to me
where Shelley is concerned.

Shelley assures me
that Claire
has a sincere affection
for me.

I respond that I
"have a very sincere
affection for my own
Shelley."

OUR CHILD TOGETHER
Autumn 1814

Shelley twists a strand
of my hair around his finger.
"I hope our child
has your fire of intellect
and your fine red hair."

I smile and slip
under his arm.
"I hope our child
has your generous spirit
and your bold ideology."

He gathers me up.
"I hope our child
has your manners
and my mayhem."

I laugh.
"I hope our child
has your passion
and my patience."

Shelley lays his hands
upon my belly
like a priest.
He whispers,
"Hello little one,
knowst thou
that you are loved,"
a prayer intoned
for the future.

OUR DAILY LIFE
Autumn 1814

We manage
this current threesome,
Claire, Shelley, and I,
by rigorous study and schedule.

In the morning
we read and write separately.
We always find funds
enough for our books.
Shelley is a devout vegetarian
and so now are Claire and I.
After our midday vegetarian meal,
we shop, visit sites of interest,
and perform house chores.
At night we either read together
or attend theater, opera, or a lecture.
Shelley teaches me Greek.
I thought that I would grow
to my greatest capacity
under my father's tutelage
and amidst his library.
But I realize even greater zeal
for knowledge with Shelley.
For on top of an education
I receive love and admiration,
and in this atmosphere
I run as a racehorse.
I pick up speed around
each new bend.

COMMUNE

Autumn 1814

Shelley talks of liberating
two of his sisters, Elizabeth and Helen,
from boarding school
so that they might
join us as we form
an association of philosophical people.

I wonder if we should not also
rescue my sister Fanny
from Skinner Street, although
it may be that Fanny prefers
a more traditional life.

Shelley writes to his friend
from Oxford,
Thomas Jefferson Hogg,
after years of no communication.
He tells him of our elopement
and of how meeting me
has changed his spirit.
He professes that he
has found contentment.
Hogg might wish to become
part of the group as well.

I grew up in a house
brimming with discussion
where Father hosted
dinners for authors,
intellectuals, and philosophers
of the day.
I would like our life
to be constructed like that.

THE RETURN OF HOGG
November 1814

Hogg supplies us with
much-needed finances
as he is to be a barrister.
And we supply him
with much-needed
intellectual stimulation.

At first I find him dull
as a spoon, but Shelley
entreats me so
to get on with Hogg
that I look to find
something in Thomas's character
I might admire.
He is for certain persistent,
and once he sheds his shyness
he holds a conversation.

Thomas seems to have taken to me
and Shelley encourages it
as Shelley's principle
of free love submits
that constancy has nothing
virtuous in itself.
I try to wrap my arms
around this concept,
but I struggle sometimes when
I hold my Shelley,
and only my Shelley,
so dear.

Apparently Hogg also
found Harriet to be entrancing
and Shelley's sister Elizabeth,
so I am not first,
just the latest
of Hogg's infatuations
with women he knows
through Shelley.

I do not harbor
feelings beyond friendship
for Hogg, but to please Shelley
I sometimes pretend to.

Thank goodness
pregnancy keeps
the possibility
of physical intimacy
with Hogg impossible.

FREE LOVE

January 1815

Winter gnarls at the door,
and I struggle to keep warm.
But the late-night talks
about spirit worlds, ghosts,
and forming an association
of philosophical people
allow me to forget
any physical discomforts
this pregnancy brings.

Claire, Hogg,
Shelley, and I
believe an ideal society
can be formed
if we free human behavior
from the restraints
of social expectations.
Shelley wants us to push
at the boundaries of monogamy,
practicing it only if
it reflects our genuine
passions and desires.
We should let loose
restrictive social conventions.
Shelley takes up the mantle
of my father, wants us to practice
what my father philosophized.

We create a small community,
we four, but a good one to build upon.
Or at least that is what Shelley
believes. I question whether
Claire and Hogg serve as worthy
members sometimes.

Hogg sends me a love letter.
Without my knowledge,
Shelley invites Hogg over
and Shelley and Claire depart
so that I might be alone
with Hogg. I try not to act
afraid or upset.

Thomas sits too close to me
as though he wishes to nest
in my lap. The silence screams.

"Thank you for the letter
and the expression of your feelings."

"I meant every word,"
he says predictably.

"At this time
I cannot fully return
your feelings
for we have known each other
such a brief time.
But I take it in good faith
that our friendship will blossom
until we are happier
than most lovers."
I rub my belly
because the baby kicks.

"I am not an impatient man."
Hogg stands up and moves
to a chair so that we face each other.
He softens his voice.
"How are you feeling today?"

"I am feeling understood,"
I say.

SHELLEY AND CLAIRE

January 1815

My Shelley nicknames me
Dormouse, Maie, and Pecksie,
after the characters
in a children's book,
but leaves me alone
as I bleed
with this pregnancy.
He and Claire roam
about town, on the walks
I should be taking,
but cannot as I am
imprisoned in bed.

I worry with silent tears
that just like Mother bled with me
my fate will be similar to hers,
and when this baby comes
I will never see my Shelley again.

One might be angry
with Shelley but I understand
that he cannot be tied down.
He is like the sun,
sometimes shining his light upon others.
And I cannot and will not expect
him to give warmth to only me.

Shelley's grandfather dies
and he is to receive
one thousand pounds a year,
one-fifth of which
will go to Harriet and her two children,
now that her Charles,
my Shelley's heir, was born.

My, up to now, silent father
calls loudly upon Shelley
to make good his promise
of support now
that Father learns
that Shelley comes
into a little money.
My father does not
seem to care
that he will soon be
a grandfather
and still will not
speak to me or see me.
I long so
to see Father,
but my father remains
walled against me.

The only constant one
is Hogg. He visits me
like a faithful pet.

MORE THAN AN ANNOYANCE
January 1815

As Claire lets out
the waist of one of my skirts
she cannot hold back
her tongue;
"I would never have
imagined how big
one becomes
when one is pregnant."

I can no longer
see my feet when
I look down.
I have noticed
that Shelley lies
farther from me in bed lately
as though he fears
touching my body.
And somehow
Claire knows it.

I think of the myriad
comments I could make
about my stepsister
and her facial features
but I just say,
"One day I hope
you experience
pregnancy and all
of its wonders too."

BIRTH
February 22, 1815

My baby comes early,
and I am at ease
when she arrives.
Shelley, agitated
and exhausted, paces
about the room.

We do not name her
as we were not prepared
for her to be born yet
and selected no name.

I am as though
the sun
ran through my body
and light
beams from my pores.
Being a mother delights me so.

Shelley and Claire
run about town for a cradle
and to find us a new home,
though I wonder if we should
move the baby.

We move on March 2
to Arabella Row.
When I awake on the eleventh day
of my little baby girl's life,
I cannot stir her.

When I went to nurse
her the night before she didn't budge
and I thought her sleeping.
She is so cold when I pick her up today
my arms ache holding her.
No breath rises in her chest.
My baby neither moves, nor screams,
nor can I.

I was a mother
and I am no longer
I was a mother
and I am no longer
repeats through my brain.

I don't know what to do
and a heavy numbness
settles over me
like one lost
out in the cold
all night.
I cannot be moved
from bed.

I send for Hogg
to help with arrangements
and to console me.
I feel I can rely on him,
and I worry
that Shelley might not handle
what is required
or my mood right now.

My own mother
died eleven days
after my birth,
and my baby
lived only eleven days.

Shelley and Claire
resume their daily schedule
of visits to money lenders
and booksellers,

but a part of me
has died.

MARCH
March 1815

I dream my baby girl
restores to life;
we rub her
before the fire
and she opens her eyes.
But then I awake
and the cradle lies empty.
And my heart shatters
all over again.

Shelley fears he is dying
of consumption.
He obsesses about death,
yet seems to forget
that we have just lost
a child.

Claire has no understanding.
"Why must you always
gloom about so?" she demands.

Claire must go.
I tell Shelley this.
I need to breathe.
I cannot even
see my own hands
when Claire stands in front of me.

We cannot send her
back to Skinner Street
as the family scandal
of us leaving with Shelley
cannot be condoned by Father
or it will damage
my sister Fanny's prospects
of gainful employment
with her aunts.

Because there is nowhere else
for Claire besides among us right now,
here she remains
like a hat pin through my skull.

But another solution
will be found.

SALT HILL
April 1815

Shelley and I travel
alone to the Windmill Inn
at Salt Hill in Buckinghamshire.
The creditors
hound my love and
we need to escape.

The inn is as pretty
as I could have imagined,
the fields greener
than emeralds,
and we steal away
from London alone,
never mind the reason.
I feel serenity and joy
for the first time
in months.

Shelley kisses me
tenderly and whispers
that perhaps we should
try to have another child.

I can think of nothing I want more.

GOOD RIDDANCE
May 1815

We return to a new house
that Hogg finds us,
and Claire tramps about the rooms
as though she is the lady of the house.
I reach wit's end.

Shelley retreats by reading Seneca,
while Claire and I
fight like angry hens
about every choice to be made.

My sister Fanny sneaks
out to see us from time to time,
though if my father
knew she saw us
he would string her up.
Her visits are brief as a glance,
and she often entreats Shelley
to give my father money
as she claims his situation to be dire.

Sir Timothy, Shelley's father,
settles Shelley's debts as well as
some of my father's obligations.
We will finally receive
our annual allowance
of one thousand pounds,
two hundred of which
go to Harriet. At long last
we shall not be
running from creditors.

Shelley spends all morning
with Claire, all afternoon
amusing her as well,
and in the evening
they share a last talk.
For tomorrow
Claire leaves for Lynmouth,
a village in Devon
on the west coast of England,
where she will reside alone.

I gavotte about the house
light as silk.

While Shelley escorts Claire
to her carriage
I await at home,
maintaining my usual schedule.

When he does not return all day
I pace the house
with tears that fail to end.
I fear that Shelley has fled
with Claire
and left me,
like he did Harriet,
for good.

TRUST
May 1815

When I lived
on Spinner Street
with nothing but my wits,
Shelley recognized
in me a glow
of greatness.

When we eloped
to Switzerland
on nothing but our beliefs,
Shelley held
my hand promising
not to let go.

When we lost
our first child
to death's cold silence,
Shelley vowed
to once again
create our family.

When I wait
in an empty house
for my love's return,
I shall be vindicated.
Shelley will bound
back into my arms
as though we never
were apart.

OUR REGENERATION

Summer 1815

Shelley more than returns
to me.
With Claire gone
we nestle into life
as a twosome.

I am pregnant
again, and happy
as my beating heart.
Health becomes paramount
as I refuse to lose this baby.
My poor Shelley
suffers from debilitating
abdominal pains
and panics that he will die
very soon of consumption.
I believe this may be somewhat
a construct of his overactive mind.

Nevertheless, we must
escape London
and salve him with the seaside.
We vacation to Clifton
and Torquay, both renown
for their health-giving air.
But my Shelley stirs, restless,
even as we travel
and abandons me
to holiday alone.
He returns to London
to seek a home for us
and to see Dr. Lawrence,
who assures Shelley
that he has not contracted consumption.
Lynmouth is less than a day's walk
from here, and I fret
when Shelley leaves me;
he does so
to visit Claire.

A HOME
August 1815

Shelley finds us a home
in Bishopsgate, near Windsor.
I love it immediately
as there is a garden
and enchanting views of the abbeys,
the heath, and the lake.
I also acquire a small staff
to perform the domestic duties
I do not adore.
We establish a routine
of reading, writing, and talking.
My hands plunged
into the earth,
cradling a book,
or even better moving
a pen across paper,
I am at home.

A MUSE

August 1815

Without Claire
I hear thoughts
as music.
My mind frees
to once again
delve into learning.
I read everything
within reach
knowing
that this prepares
me for later writing.
Shelley has picked
up his pen here
in Bishopsgate,
and he calls me
his lovely muse.

VISITORS TO OUR HOME
August 1815

Hogg visits infrequently.
Claire gratefully does not call upon us.
But Thomas Love Peacock
takes up residence in Marlow
and will make the long walk
up the Thames to stay with us
from time to time.

He advises Shelley
on his writing and career
as he is seven years his senior
and then becomes his agent
and business adviser.

We argue into the night
about vegetarianism,
the return of the French monarchy,
the disrepair of the government,
and Thomas encourages
us to read classical texts again.
Peacock convinces
Shelley to change his diet
of bread, butter, and lemonade
and finally eat a pork chop.
Shelley loses his pallid complexion
and starts to feel markedly better.

My brother Charles Clairmont
also frequents our home
as he is now free to do so.
But, to my sorrow,
Father still will not
acknowledge me.

Charles concocts many ideas
for his future, but they
all require funding from Shelley.
Thomas provides us
some relief from Charles
by chaperoning him on long walks.

One night after reading Peacock's poem
"The Genius of the Thames,"
we four decide to embark
on a boating expedition
up the river. I enjoy
the old houses surrounded by
purple loosestrife and golden water-irises.
The slow row of the boat
through the locks soothes me.
I lounge back and smell
peace in the air.

We discuss history,
politics, and literature
with vigor and ambition.
We spend the day
wandering Oxford
and stand in Shelley's
old room at University College.
Magic occurred here,
an alchemy of spirit
pushed at the boundaries
of human knowledge.
This is where my Shelley and Hogg
threatened the world
to open its eye,
and for such blasphemy
were expelled.

We travel ten days
but no more
even though we thought
to try and reach Wales
and the Lake District.
We haven't adequate funds,
and the water lowers
so shallow, we must
carry the boat
above our heads.

We merrily voyage home.

BISHOPSGATE
Autumn 1815

Shelley finds great inspiration
and harmony here
in Bishopsgate.
He embarks on a new poem
even more ambitious
than *Queen Mab*.

Peacock suggests
he call it *Alastor*
or *The Spirit of Solitude*.
It tells the story of a poet who
leaves his home
to wander the world,
and ends with the poet's solitary death
which is then mourned
by nature and the narrator.
I help him copy the poem out
and praise the work
as genius.

In *Alastor* Shelley raises the question
of whether a poet
needs companionship
or solitude to produce great work.
I am never certain
which best serves Shelley himself.

Inspired, I find that I must
study Latin again
as we have many classical
discussions, and I want
to be active in the conversation,
not just one taking notes.
I apply myself to daily exercises
and Shelley is impressed
by my quick progress.

This pregnancy feels
more stable, too,
like a boat on still water.
I begin to have faith
that the baby will be fine.

WILLIAM SHELLEY
January 24, 1816

Born this day
a baby boy.
We name him William
after my father.

I cradle my baby
in my arms
and hope that Father
will wish to do the same.
William appears healthy
and strong as the sea.
As I nurse him for
the first time
I know for certain
I wish us to never part.

Claire comes to helps me
with the birth and the baby,
but she is determined
not to stay with me and Shelley.
She seeks more independence.
This is good,
because I am determined
not to let her stay.

THE INFAMOUS POET
Winter-Spring 1816

Where Claire has lived
these past few months
seems a bit of a mystery.
She stays out of touch
until she requires something of me.

Claire writes many letters
of late, and thankfully
not to my Shelley
as in the past.
She decides to correspond
with another more infamous
and yet celebrated poet,
Lord Byron.

Much gossip
surrounds Byron
and I cannot truly distill
what is truth,
but it appears he
recently legally separated
from his wife
as he had an affair
with his half-sister.

I care little for scandal
and those who spread it;
what matters to me
is that Byron's poetry is triumphant,
faint-inducing.
I hold him in great esteem.
Still, Byron is renowned
as the most dangerous man
in Europe.

I cannot conjecture
what scheming Claire has done
to earn his favor,
but Byron asks to see
me.

I find Byron amiable, delightful even,
despite accusations to the contrary.
He is more intelligent
than are his characters
and more gentle than
his menagerie of exotic pets.
He praises Shelley's *Queen Mab*
and speaks of how he admires
my father's writings and philosophy.

It serves as a perfectly
convivial meeting,
and we pledge
to find another occasion
to share company.

But why Claire
insisted
that she arrange
this introduction now
I have yet to discover.

WHAT OF BYRON
Spring 1816

I ask Claire to explain
what is happening,
why she bid me see Byron,
the famous man,
the Napoleon of literature.
What is her connection
to him?

She hesitates
and then insists that she sought
his literary advice
about the play she is writing
and her idea to become an actress,
but I know that is not all.

Finally she says,
"You have your Shelley
and I have my Byron.
I have found a poet
to love too and he
is celebrated throughout
Europe, dear sister."
Her eyes twinkle
as she awaits my response.

"Oh Claire,
what have you done?
The man's reputation
precedes him.
He is like summer rain;
he comes and goes
as he pleases
and needs no one.
They say he loves
but one and that is his sister.
Dear Clary, what have you dug
yourself into?"

Claire fixes hard upon
my brow like she might
sear me alive.
"You and Shelley eloped
after only three months.
I have been writing
and spending time with Byron
for two. Why should you think
this would be any less
of a love affair than yours?"
She looks to stomp out
of the room, but I grasp her arm.

"No one has said that,
dear sister. I just worry for you.
Byron and Shelley
are not necessarily the same."

"I have pledged my love
to Byron and promised
that you and Shelley and I
will visit him in Geneva.
He gave me his address."

I shake my head.
I know not what plot
Claire has afoot, but I fear
it will not work as she expects.

TRAVEL ABROAD
May 1816

Claire determines
our next adventure.
And Shelley is eager to embark
on another journey.
He excites at the prospect
like a child crawling toward
his favorite rattle.

We will go to Geneva
so that Shelley
might be acquainted with
the great Lord Byron.

I weary to take William,
only five months old,
on such an excursion,
but I also believe
there might be something
of my destiny wrapped
up in Geneva, that
perhaps travel
and another meeting
with Lord Byron
may unlock some yet
untapped secret inside of me.

Shelley and I both know
that I must live up
to the standards of my birth,
after all. And I have not
been writing as much lately
with a new baby.

And because
Shelley sets his heart
upon this journey
and I cannot bear
to be without him
for a year, I must go.

After ten days of travel
through France,
by carriage not foot,
as we learned our lesson
the last voyage, we arrive
in Switzerland.

I awe once again
over the majesty of this landscape,
over its beauty and terror
like a creature otherworldly.

We arrive before Lord Byron,
but Claire pleases to note
that letters have been left
for him at the post,
so he must be on his way.

GENEVA

May 1816

We take a suite of rooms
at the Hôtel d'Angleterre
on the periphery of Geneva.

Claire cannot be contented
as she visits the post office
daily only to find that Byron
has not yet arrived.

Shelley and I feel as happy
as fledgling birds,
without a care as to what twig
we light upon. I have found new wings
here. The Alps entrance
and energize me. We rent
a small sailboat and do not
return until ten in the evening,
reading and writing all day.
We translate my father's
Political Justice into French,
and I am writing a children's
book for Father to publish.

This is the land
where Milton, Voltaire,
and Rousseau have lived.
One breathes literature here.
And I am in love with it.

THE ARRIVAL OF THE GREAT POET

May 25, 1816

Byron travels in a huge carriage
modeled after one Napoleon designed,
complete with a bed,
pulled by ten horses.
He attracts crowds along his route.
And he is rumored to have taken
a liking to a few chambermaids
during his passage. He travels
with his longtime valet, Fletcher,
and his personal physician,
John Polidori, who also has
literary aspirations and writes
an account of his travels with the great poet.

As soon as Byron arrives at the hotel,
where he signs in as being
one hundred years old, I imagine
weary from travel,
Claire besieges Byron with letters.
She follows his every move
for two days and then
accosts him as he returns
from a boat trip,
Shelley and I as unknowing
accomplices.

The great poet
and my Shelley get on splendidly
at first meeting
as if they had been childhood friends.

Byron and Shelley
look very opposite,
Shelley fair and Byron dark.
The younger Shelley frail,
while Byron at twenty-eight
stands more robust and athletic.
Shelley's voice pitches high
as a schoolboy's
while Byron's is bass and dramatic
as the scenery.
One might imagine them
to be too different to get along
and yet they seem to fit
as light and shadow.

Byron invites Shelley to dinner.
Claire and I are not to be
in attendance.

OUR GROUP OF FIVE
June 1816

Well it seems
that our community
shall be a group of five
this summer—
Shelley, Byron, Claire, Polidori,
and me.

Shelley and Byron boat
around the lake
and my Shelley tells me
how they have discussed
all manner of art, literature,
science, politics, and philosophy.
I try not to feel envy
that I spend my day
listening to Claire despair
that she has not shared
enough company with Lord Byron.
She asks me what to do
to make him desire her more,
and I scratch my head.
Her persistent cawing
does little to improve
her position I think,
but I am proven wrong
and Byron invites her
to his side one evening.

I stick firmly to my regimen
of reading and writing
to keep me sane.
My little baby
William thrives in this climate.
I feel something begin
to stir inside me here
amidst the mountains,
and it is not a child.

A STIRRING

June 1816

Like the quiet before
a storm, something
brews within me.

It is as if I awaken
from a dream
without language
into a landscape
of words.

The people
and topography,
both grand and inspiring,
envelop me.
I hear a voice
and know it to be
my own.

STORMS IN GENEVA
June 1816

We transfer from the hotel
to a waterside cottage
called Maison Chapuis
on the southern shore
where Shelley and Byron
can keep a boat.

The storms here illuminate
the sky like gods pointing
fingers of light above the earth.
The lake reflects the mountains
as the moon reflects the sun,
so brilliant in flashes of night.
The clouds cast an overall
eerie atmosphere
that excites the senses.
You smell the rain coming,
feel the thunder tremble
through you as though
you were the drum of the sky.
I have never witnessed such storms.

When the two poets
drift out on the lake
and a storm begins to blow in,
Byron sings to calm his nerves.
You can hear his voice
just above the lap of the water.

We are forced inside
most nights because
of the turbulent weather this summer.
I delight in the company
of everyone, except perhaps
Claire, although she behaves better
now that she shares Byron's bed
from time to time.

VILLA DIODATI AND THE MAN-MONSTER

June 10, 1816

Byron rents the much larger
Villa Diodati, the prettiest place
on all the lake, and just
a ten-minute walk from our house.
John Milton's schoolmate had been
Charles Diodati, so Byron loves
the villa for its literary history.

Because of Byron's reputation
he is not allowed much privacy.
English tourists rent telescopes
from the hotel to spy on him
from across the lake.
They view tablecloths on the line
as petticoats and assume
that we ladies remove our petticoats
when we accompany Byron.
He is accused of corrupting
all the ladies of the rue Basse.
Thank goodness the rain keeps
Byron and his visitors mainly indoors.

Still the rumors abound
that he sleeps with both
of the Godwin girls,
meaning Claire and me,
and that Shelley and he
have formed "A League of Incest."
This is wrong and ill
on many levels,
as none of us are related
and Byron is having an affair
with Claire alone.
Still Lord Byron
will not acknowledge her
as his mistress.

POLLY DOLLY

June 15, 1816

John Polidori appears
to have developed
feelings for me.
I view him as a younger
brother.

Today as I stroll
up the hill toward the villa,
the rain has made
the ground slick
and Byron urges Polidori
to be gallant and jump down
from the balcony and offer
me his arm. At once Polidori
swings himself over the rail,
but he slips badly as he hits
the ground and sprains his ankle
much to the delight of Lord Byron.
Byron and I aid him inside
to elevate his foot.
John blushes from embarrassment.
And it seems that Polidori
will be limping now for some time.

Perhaps Byron
should hold back his laughter
and enjoy having the company
of another who limps about
as Byron himself has one leg
shorter than the other
and always walks with a slight limp
he tries to obscure.
Of course none of us
would dare to mention it
out of courtesy and fear
that the wrath of the great Lord
would avalanche upon us.

ROUTINE
June 1816

Byron works best late into the dawn,
falling asleep as the sun seeps
into his room. He does not
awake until the afternoon,
so Shelley and I spend
mornings studying, reading,
and sailing together. We hire
someone to care for little William.

Claire is as entangled
as a fly caught in a spider's web
in her pursuit of Lord Byron.
She finds little interest
in spending time with just us.

I discover a new
rival for my lover's attention.
The men enjoy boating and speaking, alone.
Byron does not admire
the words and thoughts of a woman
as does Shelley.
He sees women more
as playthings to be used
and tossed aside
than as useful, educated minds
to be probed.

Byron directs our conversations
at night when the five
of us are driven inside
by rain and darkness.
He usually asks his questions
specifically to Shelley
as if neither Claire nor Polidori nor I
add anything
to his enrichment of the topic.

I, the ever faithful Dormouse,
listen attentively as they speak
of science and mysticism,
storing away
morsels of information
for later use.

A WATCH FOR FANNY
June 1816

Shelley and I venture
into Geneva
to find a pocket watch
for Fanny,
one that winds
and will stand
on its own
as she so often does.

She is a keeper
of the times to us
and sends us
letters of home
since our arrival here.
Sometimes a hint
of her desire to be
with us scents
the letters, but I think
she cannot imagine
being ostracized by Father.

Steady as a clock
that ticks with precision
and delicacy,
she is as golden
as the one
we select for her.

FLUTTER STORIES

June 16, 1816

Storms thrash the trees
and rain beats upon the roof
as though stones may penetrate
the ceiling. Tonight Byron
selects a volume of German ghost stories
translated into French to read to us,
stories designed to flutter the heartbeat,
so that our insides will tremble
in rhythm with the torrent outside.

The candlelight flickers
as he intones tales of twin sisters,
one of whom dies and is reanimated
and takes the place of her sister
with her new bridegroom.
Another recounts a tale
of a girl who disobeys
her father to marry a man
and then ends up losing
her baby and being abandoned
by her husband.
I delight to jump
as the thunder claps above us,
and I feel the spirit of imitation
arrive among us.

Byron suggests we each
write a ghost story,
Shelley, Polidori, Claire, he, and I.
He tells me we shall publish
ours together because I seem
particularly captivated by this contest.
I feel that he may be correct;
something besides the storm
alights my nerves this evening.
Byron says we shall see
who among us writes the best story.

CREATIVE ENDEAVORS
June 1816

I busy myself
to think of a story,
but sadly the muse does not
arrive. I want to speak
to the mysterious fears
of our nature and to awaken
thrilling horror.
Nothing comes to me.

Shelley begins a story
about the experiences
of his early life, but
abandons it because he
is more adept at embodying
the emotions and ideas
of brilliant imagery
and in writing musical verse
than in the mechanics of story
these days.

Byron sets right to work
on a story about an aristocrat
traveling in Turkey who is possessed
by a mysterious secret. But Byron
grows bored with his pages
and gives up the story,
much more at home with poetry.

Polidori, as I am,
is troubled to begin
an idea at first,
but then begins a dreadful tale
about a skull-headed lady
who is punished for peeping
through a keyhole.
I think he may have to let
the story go as it is dull
as an unsharpened knife.

Claire, I do not believe,
attempts to try to write
a story at all. She seems
content to copy out Byron's poems
for him, which I do as well,
provided I am surrounded
by lively conversation.

I will surely arrive upon
an idea for a story soon enough.
I refuse to give up.

INSPIRATION
June 22, 1816

At breakfast I am asked once again,
"Have you thought of a story?"
And I reply with an embarrassed "No."

Shelley and Byron
are planning a long boat ride
around the lake alone.
But tonight we will all
dine at the Villa Diodati.

At dinner Shelley and Byron
discuss the nature of life,
and whether there
is any probability of it ever being
discovered and communicated.
I sit quiet as a dormouse,
as does Claire. The discussion
turns to Erasmus Darwin
and how his vermicelli
in a glass began to move
with voluntary motion.
I start to wonder if a corpse
might be reanimated.
I speak none of this aloud.

Perhaps, I think to myself,
the component parts
of a creature might be manufactured
and made vital. Our conversation
continues past the witching hour
and when I retire to sleep,
I find myself wide-awake.

The room is dark as ebony,
and I close my eyes
only to have a vision
of a pale student kneeling beside
a thing he has put together—
the hideous phantasm of a man
stretched out upon a table.
The creature seems inanimate
then shows uneasy signs of vitality.
Afraid of his creation
the creator flees
to find sleep, hoping
that the hideous creature
will cease to live.
But instead the man awakes
to find the monster looming
over him with yellow, watery,
speculative eyes.

I open my eyes,
terrified of this vision
I just beheld. I try to find
something in the room
that is real so that I can
break from my reverie.

If only I can get that
hideous phantasm
to leave my mind.
If only I could think
of a story that would
scare the others as much
as this vision has scared me.

And then I realize that perhaps
I just did.

WRITING
The End of June 1816

Shelley and Byron
take flight on their boat ride
around the lake
for a week, but I
am writing my story now
and like a lioness upon
her prey cannot be diverted.

Polidori still lies up
with his ankle
and Claire acts very odd.
She and Shelley
shared a series of talks
from which I was excluded
before he left on his trip.

I should care what is afoot
but I concern myself now
more with getting my idea
down on paper.

Claire continues to copy
out the third canto
of Byron's *Childe Harold's Pilgrimage*,
and it allows her entry
into his house, but he
has grown weary of her.
You can see it in the way
he disregards her presence
as though his boot
were of more interest.

Shelley gladly does not
treat me as such, but
he does show great fondness
for Lord Byron,
and I am often barred
from their meetings.
If I had not my writing
I might feel neglected,
but my work beckons.

A TRIP TO CHAMONIX
July 1816

Shelley, Claire, and I
embark on an adventure
to view the Alps and the glaciers.
Byron elects not to join us.
He says he must stay and write,
but I believe he wishes
to avoid Claire.
We travel as a threesome
once again like
some tiresome, rickety wheelbarrow.

The river Arve is swollen
as a stuffed hog. It floods
and many roads wash out.
We must also be on the lookout
for avalanches. Shelley excites
with this sort of danger.
Claire wearies, belabored as an old dog.

Everything stands colossal here,
the country savage and lovely.
We begin our journey on horseback,
but then switch to mules
as we ascend higher
into the mountains.
The Glacier des Bossons,
my first glacier,
is so vast an ice sheet
it casts darkness
upon the water
in shapes of wicked geometry.

I hear distant thunder
and feel my first rush
of an avalanche
down the ravine
of rock beyond us.
I feel as though
I may tumble
to my peril,
but then my Shelley
clutches me close
and the snow against
my cheeks enlivens me.

Up the slopes of Montanvert
the trees have been uprooted
by avalanches. Nature rears
her awful and magnificent
head here. We reach the summit
surrounded by a world of ice,
so barren and beautiful.
I begin to cry.

Heavy rains deter us from further
travel, and we head back to our villa.
But this trip imprints upon
my spirit
and shall certainly translate
into some fodder for my pen.
I will somehow
work this landscape
into the gothic tale
I have been writing.

HAUNTING SCENERY
Summer 1816

I find that I am infusing
my gothic story
with the scenery around me
and scenery that I recall
from my reading.

My main character, Victor, is the son
of Alphonese Frankenstein,
a government official in Geneva.
Victor leaves home to attend
university at Ingolstadt in Germany
where he studies science and alchemy,
overtaken by his pursuit
of the forces that generate life.
My father set his book *St. Leon*
near Ingolstadt, renowned as
the center of the Illuminati,
a secret society
that pursued revolution
and the improvement
of the human race.
In choosing these two locales
I feel as if I am honoring
two men in my life,
my father and my Shelley.

Ingolstadt represents
the pursuit of knowledge
and glory even beyond
what may be sound,
and Geneva embodies
a home
that can be destroyed
by intense desire
for power and esteem.

SHELLEY'S BIRTHDAY
August 4, 1816

My love turns twenty-four today.
I hand-stitch a balloon
for him to release over the lake.
And so that he might witness
the beauty of his surroundings
in closer proximity,
we also purchased him
a telescope as a birthday present.

We boat out onto the lake,
balloon and telescope in tow.
I read Virgil's fourth book
of *The Aeneid* to him—
the part about Dido
and her tragic love for Aeneas.
A high wind ruins
the balloon launch
and the hot air
we use to inflate the balloon
instead causes it to explode,
like a mangled show of fireworks.
I worry this may be
some sort of bad omen.

We learn that we must terminate
our European tour for now
as Sir Timothy, Shelley's father,
is making it difficult for him
to receive the money
he should inherit
according to his grandfather's will.

Also something runs amiss
with Byron and Shelley and Claire.
They meet about some matter
and purposefully do not include me.
I feel like the girl
without an invitation to the ball
who must watch everyone else
ascend their carriages
in full party regalia.

Claire returns in torrents of tears
because Byron declares
that their affair is over,
but something else
rumbles as well.

CLAIRE'S SECRET
August 1816

Sometimes I should like to squeal
like an old teakettle
because I have been barred
from discussions, but this time
it seems more than absurd.
It hurts.

Apparently back in London
Claire became pregnant
with Byron's child.
She assures all of us
that the child can be none
but Byron's and for this
I suppose I am thankful.
She informed Shelley
of her pregnancy a month ago,
but neither of them
felt me worthy
of inclusion in the conversation.

They have been talking to Byron
who is less than pleased
about the whole matter.
Lord Byron asserts
his stature and authority
and wants to have the child raised
by his half-sister, Augusta,
the one with whom he is rumored
to be in love. But Claire wisely
convinces him otherwise,
and Byron concedes to raising
the child himself, and as his own.

Claire's motherhood must,
of course, be kept secret,
especially from her own mother,
as it would mar Claire's reputation
even further than her stature
has already been damaged
by living with us.
So Shelley and I shall be forced
to hide Claire away
while she is pregnant
and gives birth.
Claire will then be "aunt"
of her own child,
merely permitted to see
her son or daughter from time to time.

I do pity her. It is not easy
to have a baby out of wedlock,
and sometimes I wish
that Shelley were free to marry me,
but Harriet and her children continue
as background figures in our life.
Yet it must be worse
when you have a child
with someone who does not
even like you.

FRANKENSTEIN
Summer 1816

Who can say with authority
what is the balance, the alchemy,
of knowledge and imagination
that gives birth to a story?
My protagonist, Victor Frankenstein,
builds his creature of graveyard parts
before he sets out to animate it
through science. I construct
my characters beginning with people
I know and then add
or rearrange other aspects of personality
to fit my plot.
Victor wants to bestow
animation upon lifeless matter
like a god, and he learns
the limitations of such an endeavor
when he finds his creation to be hideous
and out of his control.
Does not an author
wish to do the same
with her pen?
We may think ourselves
gods of creation
from time to time,
but are we not merely
humble scholars
of the word?

TO WRITE IS TO REVISE

Summer 1816

"Writing is a calling
ordained
by the gods
of literature,
no less holy
than the martyrdom
of the saints
no less sinful
than the transgressions
of the fallen."
Shelley examines
my latest manuscript pages,
offering small corrections
in the margins,
suggesting new words
for my text.

"I am learning that
writing requires
diligence and patience,
as well as passion,
my love."
I marvel at the improvements
Shelley makes to my story
and at how easily
he edits my work.
"How can you see
so quickly where
to improve my language?"

"When the story shines
in so many places,
the few spots without glimmer
require little genius
to gloss," he says.

LEAVING GENEVA

September 1816

I have remained enchanted
these last three months,
lost in a landscape
of mountains, thunder,
ice, and wondrous writing.

Now we voyage back to England
to Bath, where Claire and I shall
live so she might reside
in fashionable seclusion,
as Claire feels entitled
to such an existence
after her affair with Byron.
But it must be a residence
where we know not a soul
for Claire shows her pregnancy
like an inflating balloon.

I take art lessons
and attend scientific lectures,
but I miss Shelley terribly
as he attends to his financial matters
in London. I contemplate
turning my story of Frankenstein
into a novel
and read the epistolary works
of Samuel Richardson
for inspiration and direction.
I also read Lady Caroline Lamb's
book about Byron for fun.
It is rife with scandal.

Finally Shelley entreats
me to come to Marlow to see him
and stay at Thomas Peacock's family home.
I might be reluctant to go
as Thomas has always championed
Harriet's cause.
I fear I may be stepping
onto unstable footing
like one on the ledge
of a rocky incline.
But I miss my Shelley so.

Claire takes charge of baby William
for a few days.
I will be free of her whining,
like a child who stubbed her toe,
about Byron and his refusal
to answer her letters.

Marlow is rural and lovely,
but Peacock acts a bit chilly
to me until we discuss politics.
England is in the midst
of the Corn Laws
and quiet revolution tints the sky.
The price of bread soars
and the poor cannot but eat cake.
Thomas mocks the situation,
but Shelley and I
feel the possibility for real change.

Shelley writes to Byron
when we return to Bath together.
He describes our life here as alluring
and content. I think Shelley
exaggerates a bit, but I am so glad
to have him beside me,
I will always applaud his notions.

We tell my family
that Claire and I live in Bath
for Claire's health,
obviously omitting the pregnancy.

Fanny, my eldest and half-sister,
quiet and melancholy,
writes to us asking for Shelley
to give my father more money
even though they know full well
that we have not straightened out
our own financial situation.
She also informs us that her aunts
have left for Dublin without her.
She will have no employment with them.
Further Fanny writes that Stepmother
has never spread scandal about us,
which I know to be false.
I find this part of Fanny's letter
to be frivolous, and not
expressive of her honest feelings,
and it upsets me.

Shelley and I resume
our schedule of reading
and writing
with the fervor of evangelicals.

FANNY'S LETTER OF OCTOBER 9
October 1816

A very alarming letter arrives
from Fanny, and Shelley
departs immediately for Bristol
to look for her. Claire and I
wait up until two in the morning
pacing the rug anxious to hear news.

At first Shelley
cannot find Fanny and has no
information. Then we learn
that Fanny has died.

I feel as though
there must be a terrible mistake
and refuse to accept it.
Fanny registered at a seaside
hotel at Swansea and took
an overdose of laudanum.

She left a note on the table
next to her body which in part reads,
"I have long determined that
the best thing I could do was to put an end
to the existence of a being
whose birth was unfortunate
and whose life has only been a series of pain
to those persons who hurt their health
in endeavoring to promote her welfare.
Perhaps to hear of my death
will give you pain, but you will soon
have the blessing of forgetting
that such a creature ever existed as . . ."
The note was torn off there
so as to obscure the author.
Left beside the body was
the gold watch that Shelley
and I brought Fanny from Geneva.
There can be no mistake.

Why exactly Fanny did this
we will never know.
It may be partially because
our aunts retracted their offer
for Fanny to live with them.
Or perhaps our mother made suicide
seem a legitimate option for one so lost.
I break down to my core.
I fall limp as though
my bones have been removed
from my body.

I should have invited Fanny to come
visit us and provided her more family.
I should have guessed at her distress.
Shelley equally feels my pain.

Father does something I do not
understand. He finally writes to me,
but it is to ask me to hide the fact
that Fanny has committed suicide.
He bids me not to go to Swansea
and "disturb the silent dead."
He believes Fanny wanted
to die in obscurity so we are
to leave her to be buried
in an unmarked grave.
He does not intend to inform
my brother Charles Clairmont
of her death for many months.
To avoid scandal
he will tell others later
that Fanny died a natural death,
from a fever on the way to Dublin.
I'm not sure that it is right,
but I do as Father bids.

Claire sheds not a tear for Fanny.
It is as though Fanny
were a stranger to her.
I wear clothes of mourning.
Without my Shelley
Fanny's fate might well
have been mine.

I find some solace
in my reading and writing,
but such a kind creature
as Fanny there will never be again.

A GOTHIC TALE
Fall 1816

The monster in my book
feeling alone and unloved
enacts vengeance
on his creator by murdering
Victor's family.
Victor's young innocent brother
and Victor's wife
lose their lives at the hands
of cruel fate.

I know all too well
the horror that it is to lose
one's sibling and one's child.
One may become
mad at the world
and the injustice of it all,
rage with fists and fury.
But eventually you must
face your own contributions
to their sad ends.

ACCOLADES AND CONTINUED ENDEAVORS

December 1, 1816

Leigh Hunt, the editor of *The Examiner*,
a London newspaper, publishes
an article called "Young Poets"
where he names Keats, Reynolds,
and my own Shelley as resurrecting
English poetry to the heights
of Milton and Spenser.
He calls them the new school of poetry,
which he claims began in excess
like most revolutions, but now
is "a real aspiration after real nature
and original fancy remains
that calls to mind
the finer times of the English Muse."
My love's work will now
gain some publicity. And Byron
had so fervently urged Shelley
that he needed publicity this summer.
I am as delighted as a kitten
licking her milk-stained paws.
A bit of sunlight seeps into
what has been darkness as of late.
Hunt and Shelley strike up
a fine friendship and Shelley
visits him.

I continue with *Frankenstein*,
sometimes with the aid of Shelley.
He smiths my language
and offers suggestions
that push the narrative forward.
More than four chapters complete,
I begin to see this book take shape,
less like the monster it describes
pieced together from scraps,
but more as something of a whole.

I dream of a home
like a proper mouse hole
where we can retire to,
that might have a river or a lake.
One that would not contain Claire.
She wears on me,
now eight months pregnant.
She feels a bit like prisoners' chains,
increasingly difficult to bear.
Claire still writes Lord Byron,
but he is more silent than Fanny.

HARRIET

December 1816

Harriet's body was discovered
floating in the Serpentine
in Hyde Park in London
on December 10.
I feel beyond remorse
and reconciliation right now.
I think that this will haunt me
for the rest of my days.
It is as though I helped
push her into the cold depths
and feel directly to blame
for some of her misery.

Harriet's last letter to her sister, Eliza
says that she forgives Shelley
and wants him to enjoy the happiness
she could not without him.
She wishes her daughter,
Ianthe, to remain with her sister.
Nothing was explicitly indicated
about her son, Charles.

Harriet said she felt so wretched and tired
and lowered in everyone's opinion
that she could not drag on
a miserable existence.
She lost hope for the future.
The coroner found
that she was again pregnant,
and the baby I do not believe
could have been Shelley's.
I wish we could have
prevented this.

Shelley takes on an attitude
much like my father did
after the suicide of dear Fanny.
He blames Harriet's family
for her problems and says
Harriet became a prostitute.
There is no proof of this,
but I do not contradict Shelley.

Shelley files to get custody
of his two children,
who remain in the care
of Harriet's sister, Eliza.
Shelley shows little promise
of gaining custody however
because we are not married.

MARRIAGE
December 30, 1816

We marry at the handsome
Wren church in London, much
to the pleasure of my father,
who now welcomes
Shelley and me back
into his Skinner Street home.
So after years of exile
now that I am married
I am once again
my father's daughter.

Whether this will strengthen
the case against Harriet's
family, the Westbrooks,
for custody of Shelley's children
remains a large question mark.

I am ambivalent as the wind
about getting married.
In one great gust I am thrilled
to be united with my love
and that my children
will now be legitimate
and my father will accept us.
But blown around in a second gale
I feel that this has come about
at too great a cost
and may be tainted
like a poison broth
from the start.

MY ESCAPE
Winter 1816-1817

My writing desk
shelters me like
a cave in a thunderstorm.

As the torrents
of life drop hail
and sleet at my door
I retreat to the world
of my story.

I find serenity
as I sculpt my plot
and search out my words.
And for a time
I forget the chaos
and devastation
that surround me.

TOGETHER
Winter 1817

Does art flourish more
when the artist works
alone in a room with
just her thoughts and her pen
and little distraction
or is it communal contribution
that births the best work?
Shelley has struggled
with this dichotomy
his whole career.
I welcome my love's
input and instruction.
I sometimes
wish for a world
with less personal turmoil
but know that
I would have less
emotional experience
from which to draw
my characters.

Shelley inserts the sentence,
"It is even possible
that the train of my ideas
might never have received
that fatal impulse which
led me to my ruin,"
into my manuscript
and the paragraph springs to life.

I wrap my arms
around his shoulders.
"That is precisely
what I intended to say,"
I tell him.

He smiles. "I know.
You left a tiny hole
for me to fill,
and I delight
in patching your garden."

ALBA
January 12, 1817

Claire gives birth today
to a beautiful baby girl
she calls Alba after
the nickname we gave
to Lord Byron, Albe (for L. B.),
when we were in Geneva.
Claire hopes this baby
will bring her closer
to Byron, but he still
sends no reply
to her letters.

Bryon acknowledges the news
of the birth through Shelley
and requests that Alba's
name be changed to
Clare Allegra Byron,
so we shall call her Allegra.

Claire takes to motherhood
like flares illuminate the sky.
She revels in every moment
of it, just as I do.

Sadly my wish for a house
absentia Claire will not be.
Shelley believes we are responsible
for Claire and her little one
and after what happened
to Fanny and Harriet
I do not offer much complaint.

We lease a house in Marlow,
just far enough away from London
to feel the countryside.
Shelley has a library, and I have a garden.
It is however not a quiet existence.
We entertain many visitors,
chief among them
the Hunts, Leigh and Marianne
and their many children,
and Thomas Love Peacock,
who has taken a liking
to Claire and proposed to her.
She turned him down flat,
even though it would be
anyone's guess what her
other prospects might be.
Unfortunately,
all her hope and ambition
is still tangled up
in Byron
like one caught
in the snares
of a bear trap.

PRETENSE
Winter 1817

Although the truth
of Allegra
is as well known
among our friends
as is her name, we act
as though the baby belongs
to someone else.
And that Claire is a maiden.

When my father
and stepmother come to call
we allege that Allegra
is a cousin of the Hunts
that Claire helps care for.

I do not enjoy
the deceit I must
employ for the benefit
of Claire. I believe this lying
digs a moat between Shelley and me
where he always bolsters
Claire's position
and protects her like he's the king
of her castle, and I play the opposition.

DEVELOPING A STORY
Winter 1817

I retreat to writing.

In my book
I selected my characters' names
as deliberately as I chose
my child's name.

Victor is a pen name Percy
used in his youth
and refers to Milton's God
from *Paradise Lost*. Frankenstein
alludes to a castle we visited
on our elopement back when
I was sixteen. William,
Victor's younger brother,
contains multiple connotations
for me from my father
to my stepbrother to my son.
William would have been my own name
had I been born a boy.
And Elizabeth, Victor's adopted sister
whom he marries, recalls
both Shelley's favorite sister
and his mother.

I base my story
on traditional gothic folklore
about the alchemist or sorcerer
who relentlessly seeks knowledge
that would best remain unknown,
where the ego of the sorcerer
leads to his downfall.

I explore the renewal of life
as I would wish
more than anything
to have my baby, my sister,
my mother, and Harriet brought
back to me, but science
like a foundling branch
reaches only so far.
I also try to investigate
how sometimes
that which we create
can destroy us
or those we love.

ALBION HOUSE
March 1817

As we now receive
an annual income
from Shelley's inheritance
we renovate a new home
on West Street in Marlow
called Albion House.
With five large bedrooms,
a fir-shaded garden,
and a library that houses
all of our books
and two full-sized statues
of Venus and Apollo,
our home is blessed with love and poetry.

I labor on the final
chapters of *Frankenstein*.
The novel takes
hold of me like a carriage
drawn by wild horses.
I cannot stop its progress.
It is now a story within
a story within a story.

The manuscript grows
to novel length this way,
and I also distance myself
a bit from some of the emotion,
as the characters sat a little too close
to the real people in my life.
All three of my storytellers
are male. The first, Robert Walton,
is an explorer seeking to reach
the North Pole. He writes letters
to his sister about saving Victor Frankenstein,
the doctor who has animated a creature
from grave-stolen body parts.
When Walton meets Victor,
Victor pursues his Creature
to the end of the earth.
Victor then recounts
his story to Walton
and finally within Victor's tale
is the story narrated by
the monster himself,
the tale of the monster's plight.
I am encouraged
by the progress of the novel
and think I see my way
to the light of the end.

CHILDREN
March 1817

I am pregnant again,
the baby due
at the end of the summer.
The idea of increasing
my family pleases me
like one who does not realize
she is hungry but then
when presented with a well-prepared feast
relishes in the food.
It also inspires me to finish
my book before the baby's arrival.

Shelley loses his custody
fight for his children by Harriet,
but so do the Westbrooks.
Charles and Ianthe are assigned
neutral guardians by the courts.
Shelley is required to send them money
and is granted visitation.
My love's heart pains
over this decision,
but then he seems
to forget his first two children
almost as if they have died.
He will never again visit them.

I cannot understand this
as I would rather
cut off my tongue and give up writing
than be separated
a day from my own child.

MY BOOK
April 1817

To write a book
for me is as to finally
truly breathe,
my senses
engaging with the world.

I cannot be assured of
exactly what I created
be it madness and monster
or beauty and light,
but I tried to apply both
what I have learned
and read and observed
and that which
I can only imagine
and think and dream.

And more
than anything
I want to make
my father
proud.

THE END
May 1817

I end my book
with these lines,
"'But soon,' [the monster] cried,
clasping his hands,
'I shall die, and what
I feel will no longer be felt;
soon these thoughts—these
burning miseries will be extinct.'
. . . [The monster] sprung
from the cabin window . . . ,
and I soon lost sight of him
in the darkness and distance."

Shelley grasps my hand
as he reads my final words.
"The ending is the hardest part.
To leave behind a book
can feel as though
you separate a portion
of your heart
from your chest.
But my love,
what you have written
is majestic.
You have served
your name well."

SUMMER

Summer 1817

Now that I have finished a draft
of *Frankenstein*
and must send it to publishers,
I endeavor to go through
the journal Shelley and I kept
describing our elopement together
in 1814. I keep my mind
engaged in writing so I do not
worry about whether or not
Frankenstein sees print.
I call this new work
History of a Six Weeks' Tour.
It should be easier to publish
as travel books are very popular.

Shelley becomes known
as the town eccentric this summer,
not because he gives blankets
and food and money to the poor,
but because he tutors a village girl, Polly Rose.
His quirky ways of oratory
where he flails his arms around
caught up in the rapture of his ideas
frighten some of the locals.
I adore when he gets
that fire in his eyes
and his emotions
bubble over the surface.

Claire still pines after Lord Byron
like the starving eye chocolate
and only her child seems to quench
her despair over him.

My pregnancy causes
me no troubles, thank goodness.
I grow excited for the new baby.
I nest as any proper mother would,
preparing space in our home
for its arrival, readying the nursery
like a bird gathering twigs,
and putting all of my literary tasks
in order.

A PUBLISHER

Late Summer 1817

At the end of the summer
I find a small publisher
who will bring out five hundred
copies of *Frankenstein*
in the late winter.
The book will be published
anonymously,
with Shelley writing the preface
and referring to his friend
as having written the book.
As I have no stature
it would only damage the book
to attach my somewhat
notorious name to it.
Because of his contribution,
even uncredited, it may
be assumed that Shelley
wrote the book.
Still I elate; the book
that Shelley nurtured with me—
my first literary endeavor—
will be published.
This book will be born.

ANOTHER BIRTH
Autumn 1817

On the second of September
I give birth to a baby girl
we name Clara Everina,
after Claire and my mother's sister.
I am exhausted after this birthing
and can't seem to produce
enough milk for the baby.
I refuse to have a wet nurse though.
My mother thought
that sort of child rearing
a bad idea, so I struggle
like a mother bird
in the depth of winter
to feed my child.

William seems very susceptible
to the cold here this autumn,
and yet I will not ask Stepmother
to send the flannel I require for him
as she has once again been difficult,
angered like a jealous suitor
by my father's visits
to see me.

Claire and Shelley live in London
part of the time, and I am alone
with the children like a nanny.
Shelley complains of bad health
as he did after the births
of each of our children.
I can't fathom why
he must go through
such antics after I give birth.
Perhaps he feels
sorry that he did not
have to go through
the pain of labor
and so contracts
his own feelings of distress.

I thought maybe my dear
childhood friend Isabella
might once again contact me,
but her husband, Mr. Booth,
ends that possibility
and spreads rumors that
Claire and Shelley
are having an affair,
and further that Allegra
is Shelley's child.

We mire ourselves
in debt again.
Shelley is arrested
because we cannot pay
all of our bills.
What shall I do if he
and I truly part?

He urges me to come
to London, but I fear
that like in Bishopsgate
if I leave the house abandoned
all of our property will be seized.
And we have so much more to lose now.

November brightens my spirit
as I let go my fears
and agree to travel
to London to be with my Shelley.
I visit Skinner Street
and the Hunts.
Also *History of a Six Weeks' Tour*,
my first book, appears this month,
again with an anonymous author.

ANONYMITY

Autumn 1817

Notoriety a distant dream
as scandal brands us
notorious,
I think that when
I can name myself
I shall use
Mary Wollstonecraft Shelley
in memory of my mother.

If I were a man
I might not wear the cloak
of anonymity.
The temperamental child
inside me
pounds her fists
in anger about this,
but the wiser, patient Mary
just keeps writing
without a name.

BYRON'S REQUEST
Autumn 1817

Byron demands that we send
him his daughter.
He does not quite grasp
that shuttling a nine-month-old
off to Italy with strangers
might not be the greatest plan.
Still I will be glad to be done
with the scandal that has been caused
by having little Allegra around.

Claire will no doubt
act more sullen and complaint heavy
than she already behaves
without her little one.
But she should have known
when she became involved
with Byron
that there would be
a Faustian cost,
that she would barter away
part of her soul.

THE RELEASE OF
FRANKENSTEIN
January 1818

Even though only five hundred copies
are published, some note
is taken of my book.
My friends shower me with praise
for my imagination and bold ideas.
The outside world
of course does not know
who authored *Frankenstein*,
only that the preface
seems masculine
and that the book is dedicated
to William Godwin,
my father.

If I receive no admiration
beyond that of my father
it would be more than enough.
He wrote that *Frankenstein*
is "the most wonderful work
to have been written
at twenty years of age
that [he] has ever heard of."

The reviews I am told
are happily mixed.
I do not read them
as we are preparing
to leave for Italy
to transport Allegra to Byron.
And honestly I can weather
no negativity at the moment.

We find someone
to take on the twenty-one-year lease
we made for Albion House.
I feel torn about leaving.
The weather chills the bones
and Shelley has been very sick here,
now with an eye infection
that makes it impossible
for him to read. However,
we took up residency here
and it was refreshing
to have a permanent address
in the country. I finished
my book in this house.
My daughter was born here.
It feels bittersweet to leave.

RUMORS AND TRUTH

February–March 1818

I board up Albion House
and join Claire, Shelley,
and the children in London.
I detest our current lodgings
but we could find nothing else.
We cannot stay at Skinner Street
as there is once again
turmoil over finances
like angry bulls huffing in a pen.

Shelley took out another
post obit loan, promising
forty-five hundred pounds
on his father's death
for the receipt of two thousand now.
My father expected to receive
a good portion of that money.
I try not to enmesh myself
in money issues as I find it
a cemetery for creativity,
but I am not sure
how Father will get along
without Shelley's help.
We can always just borrow more.

We delve into culture
and entertainment,
spend many nights with the Hunts.
We see the Elgin Marbles,
an exhibition of Salvador Rosa,
and the Appollonicon, an organ that sounds
like an orchestra. A large scenic view of Rome
makes us hunger for our trip abroad.

But rumors cast a pall
over our last days
in England. Word reaches
Stepmother and Father
that Allegra is Claire's child,
and that Shelley is the father.
We explain that Lord Byron
is in fact the father of Allegra
and that we are taking
Allegra to him.

Stepmother yells,
"Claire's downfall is all
the result of her following
you into hell, Mary,"
as if I had anything
to do with Claire courting Byron.
But Stepmother
must point blaming fingers
at me as she did when
I was a child in her house.

HEAVEN OR HELL
March 1818

If there were but one
way to construct a life
perhaps the road
would be easier
for having no choice
of left or right,
but as freethinking
individuals we make
decisions.

I never chained Claire
to my leg.
She rides in the carriage
designating her own seat.
No road without gravel
and dust, no course
without twists,
the way is not always
smooth.
But the path has been
Claire's choice,
and I respect her for it.

A LETTER FROM CLAIRE TO BYRON

March 1818

Claire writes to Byron
of *Frankenstein* and me,
"Mary has just published
her first work . . . a wonderful
performance full of genius
. . . as no one would imagine
could have been written
by so young a person.
I am delighted and whatever
private feelings of envy
I may have at not being
able to do so well myself yet
all yields when I consider
that she is a woman
and will prove in time
an ornament to us
and an argument in our favor.
How I delight in a lovely woman
of strong and cultivated intellect.
How I delight to hear
all the intricacies of mind
and argument hanging on her lips."

I blush and thank her
for her kindness
and we share a true
moment of conviviality
as though the years
of swatting at each other's hats
have been but child's play.

TRAVELING TO ITALY
March–April 1818

Much of the scenery
reminds me of Geneva
as we approach Italy
traveling through France.
Once again Shelley and I
pen a joint journal of our travels.

We arrive at lovely Milan,
everything here superior
to that in France, even the oxen
that pull the peasants' carts
are as beautiful
as wild stallions.
We attend the opera
and ballet at La Scala,
the boxes so elegant
a queen would feel at home.
We spend three weeks
in Milan expecting Lord Byron
will soon accompany us
and collect little Allegra,
who is now fifteen months old
and showing the personality
of a blooming rose.

Shelley and I take a trip
to Lake Como by ourselves,
and search out a house
that might tempt Byron
to stay on with us for a while.
Unfortunately no houses
are available. I love the escape
with my Shelley, and the sweet-scented
myrtle and tall cypresses
enchant me as though we are
part of a fairy story.

House or no house,
Shelley nevertheless writes
and invites Byron to come
and spend the summer
on the lake with us.
Byron responds rather coldly
that he has no intention of leaving Venice
and that a messenger will be sent
to collect Allegra, as if Allegra
were some package. Further,
Claire is told that all contact
with Allegra will cease
from this point forward.
Claire cannot be consoled at first,
and Shelley and I perplex over
how to handle her.
When the messenger arrives on April 22,
we tell Mr. Merriweather
that Allegra is sick and cannot be moved.

Rumors abound
that Byron leads a scandalous
life in Venice, and Shelley
troubles over what to do
with Allegra. He offers to keep
the child as part of our family.
I do not find this to be a good solution.
I instead propose that Elise,
our wonderful nursemaid,
be sent to stay with Allegra
as she herself is a mother
and can report to us
about Allegra's welfare.
Claire agrees to this.
On April 28 Allegra,
Elise, and Mr. Merriweather
set out for Venice.

MEETING MARIA GISBORNE

May–June 1818

Because no house can be
found for us on Lake Como,
we travel to Pisa. I climb
the 224 steps
to the top of the leaning tower
only to witness just how
fully the city declines.
The cobblestone streets
sprout with weeds and grass
like a patchy beard.
Chained prisoners
street-clean, watched over
by armed guards. It reminds
one of slave labor.

Elise writes that she and Allegra
safely arrive in Venice,
and that all the Byronic rumors exaggerate.
Claire exhales a bit.

We decide to move
on to the port town of Livorno,
where my father wrote us
an introduction to Maria Gisborne.
We have acquired no new friends
on our journey thus far,
and I hunger for conversation
like one in solitary confinement.
I am especially eager to make
the acquaintance of Mrs. Gisborne
as she cared for me and Fanny
after my mother's death
when I was a baby.

Henry Reveley, Maria's grown-up son,
develops a fondness for Claire,
and we are invited to stay
on with them for a month.
Claire has yet to return
the gracious kindness
that men show her
as though any man but Byron
is but a lowly cow
and Byron a godly bull.

A pattern of communal daily
activities emerges, and I feel
at home here. In the morning
Claire and I practice our Italian.
In the evenings we walk with
the Gisbornes and Shelley,
discussing the day's reading.
I believe I have found
a true friend and motherly mentor
in Maria Gisborne.
I feel fortunate,
as though I have come
into an inheritance of my own.

BAGNI DI LUCCA

Summer 1818

Shelley finds us a house
in a spa town sixty miles
north of Livorno, Bagni di Lucca.
Casa Bertini is a small colorful building,
freshly painted, newly furnished,
and encircled by woods, mountains, and walks.
A small garden
and an arbor of laurel trees
landscape the lawn
so thick the sun cannot penetrate them.
We enjoy watching the fireflies
pattern the night sky
like little explosions
of electricity.

I receive a copy of Sir Walter Scott's
kind review of *Frankenstein*.
He praises the book
but believes Shelley to be the author.
This somewhat disturbs me,
a tiny splinter under my skin.
So I send him a letter of appreciation
and I inform him
that it was not my husband's,
but my juvenile effort.

I immerse myself
in reading and studying
English and Italian
poetry and history here.

Shelley struggles a bit,
restless as one confined
to bed. He wanders
the woods and pools, looking for escape.
He cannot find inspiration
to compose anything original here,
but instead beautifully translates Plato's *Symposium*.
We receive word from Peacock
that Shelley's name has been
linked to Leigh Hunt's in an unflattering
review of Hunt's book *Foliage*.
Shelley becomes desolate
as driftwood
and misses his friends.
He and Claire grow ever close,
and there is little I can do
to halt it.
Now that Allegra is away
all of Claire's attention
focuses entirely upon my Shelley.
It is as though
her telescopic eyes
see nothing but him.

THIEF
Summer 1818

If Claire falls into
the ocean and calls
for my rescue,
I dive into the cold
and pull her to shore.
And yet my stepsister
sees nothing wrong
with stealing from me
the lifeboat
that keeps me adrift,
my Shelley's time
and affection.

She acts as if
I cry no tears,
feel no loss.
When she sees
my wet handkerchief
for whom does
she believe I mourn?

ORPHEUS AND EURYDICE

Summer 1818

Shelley strokes my head
as we lie in the grass of the arbor.
"If as in the myth of Orpheus
and Eurydice you were
bit by vipers and called
to your death, I would
use all my powers of music
and poetry to get you back."

"You would no doubt
charm the gods
with your voice."
I clutch my love's hand
with authority.

"The way the story
would change is that
when I retrieved you
from the underworld
I would not look behind me
to check if you were there.
I would know for certain
that you would follow me.
And thereby I should
never lose you, my dear."

I look closely into
the soft blue of his eyes.
"You are right;
you shall not lose me.
I should likely follow
you anywhere."

NEWS FROM BYRON
August 1818

We receive two letters
from our former nursemaid Elise
about Allegra. The most
alarming information
is that Allegra has been
moved out of Byron's home and Elise's care
and sent to live with the British consul,
Mr. Richard Hoppner.
Elise rumors also that Byron
intends to debauch his own
daughter when she becomes
old enough and make her
his mistress, but this cannot,
of course, be substantiated.

Claire breaks dishes
and screams vengeance
like a madwoman. She vows
to leave immediately for Venice
to reclaim her daughter.

Shelley makes her calm
and will intercede on her behalf
and visit Byron instead.

Claire of course listens
to my Shelley
as he is once again
the god in her life.
But she must accompany
him on his trip.

Claire and Shelley
depart on the seventeenth
for the Hoppners' to assess
Allegra's condition.

I write to the Gisbornes
to beg them come and visit
as I will be desolate here
without my Shelley
with just the servants and children.

TRAVELING TOWARD BYRON
August 1818

Shelley writes that Allegra
remains as beautiful as ever
only taller and more pale,
but in all ways fine like porcelain.
Consul Hoppner advises Shelley
not to tell Byron
that Claire stays in Venice
as Byron often expresses
his extreme terror
of meeting her again.
For seeing Claire
might send Byron
into convulsions and panic
as though Byron suffered heart pains.

Shelley alone visits Byron
at three in the afternoon
as Byron should have risen by then.
Shelley shudders and shocks
that Byron looks older and fatter
and that he is involved in all
forms of debauchery.
This explains why
Byron does not want to see
old friends or former lovers.

Still Byron and Shelley
get on famously, riding
along the beach discussing
literature and life.
Shelley lies and says
that Claire and the children
and I are all in Padua.
Byron then invites us
to stay in Este at his summer home.

Shelley desires that I bring
the children and his servant, Paolo,
to Este in an arduous manner
and make the trip in only five days.

The visiting Gisbornes see that
Clara suffers from the heat
and is not well enough to make
the journey right now.
Only one, she cuts
her teeth with the turmoil
of one growing a horn
out of her head.
Still, we do as my Shelley bids.

The day after my twenty-first birthday
we set out for Este.
Clara never ceases crying,
and she contracts dysentery.
When we arrive in Este,
she spasms and convulses
like the monster
awaking in my book.

Claire is also mysteriously
unwell, and Shelley seems
more concerned about Claire
than his daughter. He tells
me to take Clara to Claire's
doctor's appointment in Padua
and he returns to Venice.

We set out at half
past three in the morning,
Shelley meets us in Padua
and finally recognizes how
ill little Clara has become.
He rushes Clara and me
back to Venice and leaves
us at an inn while he searches
out a good doctor. The baby
shakes and cries in my arms.
She boils with a temperature
hotter than the molten core of the earth.
I can do nothing to calm her
until she finally calms herself
and breathes no more.

MELANCHOLIA
Autumn 1818

Sadness a choke hold
around the throat,
everything fails,
tastes bitter.

I try to dismiss the blame
I feel well up inside of me,
but sometimes
I am a pot of anger
boiling over the rim.

Mostly I feel tired.
I have not the energy
to smile or frown or speak.
I bury my head in books
but want little to do
with company.
I sometimes even despair
staying too close to my son,
that he too might be snatched
soon from me.

DISTRACTION
Autumn 1818

Lord Byron gives me
some of his poems to transcribe.
He attempts to take
my mind off the loss
of my daughter.

Mrs. Hoppner and I
visit the library
and an art gallery and go shopping.

Shelley begins a new
poetic drama, *Prometheus Unbound*.

I find little distraction
in every day; even my reading
suffers attention.

I watch Claire delight
in Allegra these two months
in Este, and my heart
aches for my baby Clara
like a thousand knives
have been thrust upon me.

I cannot be intimate
with Shelley right now,
but then fear he seeks out Claire.
I do not know where
to shelter my grief.

THEN THERE ARE DAYS
Autumn 1818

A glance from Shelley
across the supper table
expresses not only concern,
but adoration—
a cherished look I remember
from our first meeting.

Claire, William, and I
collect flowers in the garden
and I witness my child's
amazement at
simple color and fragrance.

And there is the sustenance
of my books
and my journals
and my letters to friends,
the warm candlelight
of these witching hours.

THE BABY OF NAPLES
November 1818–February 1819

We decide to travel
to Naples by way of Rome.
Claire, Shelley, William,
Elise, our nursemaid, another nanny,
and Paolo, Shelley's manservant,
and I reach Rome on November 21.
We find the city casual
and under excavation;
still it enchants us
like a love story.

Shelley travels ahead of us
through the dangerous Appian Way
so that he can locate a house
for us in Naples on the Riviera di Chiaia,
the most expensive street of villas
in all of Europe.
We manage a frightful crossing,
but arrive in Naples safely.
I fill with excitement
for Naples is the home of Virgil,
and the birthplace of Latin literature.

We luxuriate in Naples,
a city of Goodness
until we find out
that Paolo has been
cheating us out of money
and impregnated Elise
our nursemaid.
They get married
and are dismissed
from our service.
The drama leaves me sleepless
and angry as a tiger
with a toothache.

Then to add to the madness,
Shelley presents me
with a two-month-old child
named Elena Adelaide
whom we must register
as being born to me and him
on December 27 of last year.
I have never seen nor heard
a whimper from this baby's mouth.

Percy brought me this baby
as a replacement
for my dear Clara Everina,
saying that Elena was a foundling
that he wanted to adopt.
But I somehow wonder
if perhaps Elena is not
really Shelley's child
by another woman.
Either way, she cannot
replace my little girl.

We leave tomorrow for Rome,
and I insist that we leave
baby Elena behind
in the care of foster parents.
I will not replace
my child like
she is a lost garment.
I cannot easily be warmed
by a newfound fur.

SOMEONE ELSE'S BABY
February 1819

Sometimes I wonder
if Shelley would not
like to father the world.
His spirit is so generous
and all encompassing.

I have lost two little girls
of my own, the weight
of those losses heavier
than Atlas shouldering the earth.

We see many things
at eye level, Shelley and me,
but a new baby not our own
I cannot bear.

ROME
March 1819

It is difficult to capture
the exact beauty
and the rich history
of this place, Rome.
It is, as Shelley says,
"a city of palaces and temples
more glorious than those which
any other city contains, and that of
ruins more glorious than they."
Shelley invites both Hunt and Peacock
to join us in Italy as he is like a knight
without his steed, so very lonesome
for his friends.

I am gladly pregnant
again and due in November.
I take drawing lessons
and write. I practice
my Italian at evening *conversaziones*
and find that Claire, Shelley, and I
get along with the language
whereas most other English
do not even try to speak it.

Shelley writes *The Cenci*
and *Prometheus Unbound*,
a work of tremendous effort
that may be the best thing
he has ever created.

Some days darken me still
like a blindfold knocking
out all sun. Shelley wishes
to return to Naples
to retrieve the baby Elena.
My father harrows
in money problems once again
and sends distressing letters.

I juggle my moods
by engaging in projects
and enjoying the scenery
stuffed with statues.
William and I tour
the sights of Rome by carriage.
We recline in the gardens
of the Villa Borghese
and try just to breathe.

WILLMOUSE
May–June 1819

The artist Amelia Curran
paints a beautiful portrait
of my blue-eyed, chubby,
but serious little William.
He chatters away now
in English, Italian, and French.
We delight to find
that Amelia has been living
in Rome the past couple of years.

She warns us that the Corso,
where we are living now,
is no place for a small delicate child
like Willmouse as malaria season
approaches, so we move
into rooms next to Amelia
on the Trinità dei Monti.

On the twenty-third of May
little William falls ill
with worms,
according to Dr. Bell's diagnosis.
He suggests that we leave Rome
because the oppressive heat
could be damaging to William.
For once Shelley
is not keen on travel.
Over a week later
William feels not better;
in fact, he shakes
with a high fever
that reminds me of his sister, Clara.
I fear the worst—
like a prisoner awaiting the guillotine.

We sit at William's bedside.
I cannot sleep.
The misery of these
hours is beyond calculation
as the hopes of my life
bind up in William.

He contracts malaria
and dies at noon on June 7.
I feel as though
my happiness ends
by the ragged edge of a blade.
I have lost three children now.

MY SELFISH ILL HUMOR
Summer 1819

I feel that I may not be fit
to live. Had I not
this baby kicking inside me,
my grief might throw
me over a cliff.
What kind of mother
sees three children die?

Father sends me a letter
expressing that if I do not quit
my selfishness and ill humor
my friends and family
will cease to love me.
So I have lost my child
of three. Does that mean
all that is beautiful
in the world is now dead,
that everything else
which has claim upon my kindness
ceases to exist? My shoulders
cave in to read his words.

SOME SOLACE
August 1819

We receive letters from
the Hunts and Hogg and Peacock
and Maria Gisborne,
all with consoling words
about my little William
and concern for me.
I cannot cheer,
but I do feel cared for,
and loved even at my lowest.

Frankenstein, I hear
through letters, despite
some less than laudatory
reviews, is still being read
and discussed in England
after it is known that
I authored it. Discussion
means that it provokes thought
and creates some controversy.
I am fueled now
by more than
just my pregnancy to carry on.

I retreat like a soldier
without weapons
to the solace of work.

I begin a new journal
on Shelley's birthday.
I also start a new novel
that I finally decide
to title *Mathilda*. It centers
around a relationship
between a father and a daughter
where the father commits
suicide and the grief-stricken
daughter cannot share
her anguish with anyone
because her father's love
for her was incestuous.

PERCY FLORENCE
November 1819

We relocate again,
this time to Florence
so that I can be in the care
of Doctor Bell when I deliver
my new baby.

The labor goes easy
and lasts but two hours.
The baby looks robust and healthy
with a nose that promises
to be as big as my father's.
I thrill to once again
be a mother,
but fear like one
about to walk a plank
that there may be
shark-infested waters
ahead of me,
that I may also lose this child.

It has been five miserable months
without a baby
and now I walk
until my feet blister
because I believe
that will help me
produce enough milk
to feed my little one.

Shelley worries over my
state of mind still,
but a little less now
that baby Percy has come.
He pleads with Maria Gisborne
to visit us, but she cannot come.
I think Shelley requires
some new companionship
but we are considered
to be radical and therefore
somewhat outcast by many people
wherever we land.

RADICAL LOVE

December 1819

Shelley says to me,
"Our love is radical
in all its definitions.
It is both
fundamental
and favoring social reform.
So when people
call us radicals
I think perhaps
they know not entirely
of what they speak."

I hold little Percy
to my breast and proclaim,
"I am proud to live
our beliefs."
Though sometimes when Claire
crawls under my skin
I favor the fundamental
portion of being radical.

"You are my core, Mary."
Shelley cups his hand
over his son's head,
and I can hardly contain
my joy.

PISA
January 1820

So that we will have
a milder climate
and can be under the care
of a better doctor
we move down the Arno to Pisa.
I find the town drab
and the Italians here shabby
as well-worn boots.

Claire and I fight daily
as though to quarrel is to breathe.
She has not seen her daughter
for far too long and we haven't
word of Allegra for months now.
Claire acts as if it is the same
as having lost a child.
I know this to be false
and find her whining more intolerable
than if she lit me on fire.

DISTRESSING NEWS
Spring 1820

We learn that Lord Byron
now lives in Ravenna
as the acknowledged escort
of Teresa Guiccioli.
He dwells in her household
along with her husband
and so now does Allegra.
Claire writes to ask
if she might not see her daughter
as it has been over a year
since she laid eyes upon her.
Byron does not respond.
And when Claire suggests
that Allegra summer with us in Pisa,
Byron questions what kind
of parents Shelley and I make
with our godlessness,
the return of our vegetarian diet,
and worse than that
the loss of our children.

He will keep Allegra with him
or send her to a convent.
Claire frenzies herself with anguish.

I think Byron ought not point
accusations of blame
unless he himself lies beyond
reproach.

Paolo, Shelley's former manservant,
blackmails my husband over Shelley's
relationship to Elena Adelaide,
the baby from Naples that we left
in foster care. We hire a lawyer
to intercede for us
and stop the blackmail,
but we must also leave Pisa for now
and travel to Livorno
to stay at an empty house
the Gisbornes have there.

My little Percy suffers
and I blame myself
and my lack of producing
good milk for him.
All of these stressful events
create a drought in me.

My father insists that he
be sent more money,
and I cannot even manage
to read my mail.
I ask Shelley to sift through it
for me and read me only
the cheerful sections.

WITH AND WITHOUT CLAIRE

August 1820

We move again to a village
four miles east of Pisa
at the beginning of August.
Thanks to the prescription
of a mild climate,
calm life, and no medicine,
my Shelley finds himself
in good health and humor.
My spirits will be raised
if Claire retreats
from us for a spell.

At the end of August
my wish is granted.
Claire goes to Livorno for a month.

Unfortunately something shifts
between my love and me.
Shelley shelves the deaths
of our three children
as if they are events from a book
he long ago read.
He seems to feel that I spoil
little Percy and fret over him
like a servant fusses over a prince.

Shelley also decides that we must
cut my father out of our lives,
for the time being, as Father
sends such upsetting letters
once again demanding money.
Further, Father and Stepmother
spread gossip about us to the Gisbornes.
Maria Gisborne now refuses
my calls. But what frightens
me the most is that Shelley
and I find a river between us lately.
One I cannot wade across
where the rapids threaten
and the water deepens.

LEARNING TO SWIM
Autumn 1820

My little Percy splashes
about in his bath,
creating tidal pools
on the floor.

I have given him
a tiny paper boat
to float on the water,
but mostly he chews upon it.

I tell Shelley I want
to take lessons
to learn how to swim properly
as we spend
so many hours
on the river and at sea.
"I want to be able
to teach Percy to swim
when he is old enough."

I dry the baby off
and find Shelley
immersed in his reading.
"Did you say something?"
he asks me.

CLAIRE IN FLORENCE
October 1820

Claire moves to Florence
and stays as a paying guest
in the home of a doctor,
Antonio Bojti.
The Bojtis require help
with many small children
and in exchange Antonio's wife
teaches Claire
to speak German.
The Bojtis also introduce Claire
to their socially well-placed friends.
She makes a good hand
out of bad cards I think
in this arrangement.
We hope that Claire
will miss Allegra a little less
being surrounded by children
and also that she will learn
to become a governess
and thereby become
more independent.
Until then Shelley,
of course, takes care
of her expenses.

Shelley accompanies
Claire on her trip
to Florence, and
I worry that he enjoys
being with her more
than he does me.

I delve into my new novel,
Valperga, which is set
in fourteenth-century Lucca, Italy.
The book describes the intellectual
and libertarian possibilities
of the nation-state.
I incorporate much research
into this book.
I find it challenging and
feel I engage all parts of my brain
even more than I have in the past.
It is as though my zest for knowledge
intersects, like lines that were once
more parallel but now meet on a grid,
with my ability to imagine.

CLAIRE FOR A MONTH
December 1820

Claire will be joining
us for Christmas, a gift
I did not ask for.

I begin to feel
at home in Pisa; the weather
even in the winter feels
like spring. And the grand duke
of Florence visits in the winter,
making Pisa a center
of fashion, interest, and culture.

I wear my hair up
in combs now.
But even though
I am careful to sport
dresses of style
in pink stripe or light color,
Shelley seems not
to notice me at all.
If he wants adventure,
he invites
Claire to be his partner.

RESEARCH
Winter 1821

The excavation of facts
satisfies me as does
hoeing my garden.
After I pick through
the unnecessary information
a story begins to emerge
as a bed of flowers
blossoms once the weeds
have been cleared.

I immerse myself
in Italy's past
in this book, *Valperga*,
and thereby
connect more
to the place I live now.

JANE AND EDWARD

Winter 1821

Thomas Medwin,
Shelley's cousin who has
lived in Pisa with us
since October, introduces
us to his English friends
Edward Williams
and his unofficial wife, Jane.
Thomas and Edward
served together in India.

I am not entranced
by Edward's military exploits,
though he boasts about them often,
but more by his love affair
with Jane, which mirrors my own.
Jane at sixteen married
a nasty naval captain
from whom she separated
the next year. Shortly afterward
she fell in love with Edward.

It was a mad love affair
like two hummingbirds
meeting midflight.
Jane broke convention
and left England as Edward's wife
even though no divorce
officially happened.
They lived in Geneva
as had Shelley and I
and bore a son, Edward Medwin,
named for their best friend.
Jane now expects her second child
in March.

Jane is pretty,
but rather unremarkable,
like a boiled egg,
except for her musical talent.
Edward shows some promise
as an artist, but is not
our usual caliber of friend
in intellectual rigor.
Still I enjoy their company
and especially Edward's
naval expertise.

INFLUENCE
Winter 1821

New friends enrich
our lives as does discovering
a new path into town.
Sometimes the road
proves preferable;
sometimes it is more rocks
and mud.
Either way you encounter
different views,
discover alternate
ways to experience life,
and learn capabilities
and vulnerabilities within
yourself yet unknown.

My circle of friends
widens and constricts
depending upon where we reside.
I sometimes long
for the sphere of influence
I found in England.

Lately I often engage
most intimately
with the research for my book.

BYRON AND ALLEGRA
March 1821

Byron enrolls Allegra
in a convent at the beginning
of the month.
Claire is so furious
she foams as a rabid dog;
she mutes beyond speech,
though not so beyond
speaking her mind
that she writes
Byron a scathing letter.
Because Lord Byron
promised that he would
raise Allegra himself
or at least until she was seven,
Claire decides she will
set Bryon straight.

Shelley and I unite
over the idea that Byron
should have the right
to send his daughter
to a convent and bid Claire
to write an apology come April.

SAN GIULIANO

Spring 1821

We rent a new Prini house
at San Guiliano,
with the Williamses
nearby.

Shelley writes a poem
to honor the dying John Keats
called *Adonais*.
I still labor to finish *Valperga*.
As two writers,
we ripen in Italy
as does the local flora.

As a couple, though,
we coast apart
as birds fallen
out of their migratory pattern.
I watch the love
between Jane and Edward
and wish to recapture
that exuberance with my Shelley.

I feel that my concern
for our child distances
me from Shelley;
even my writing
now seems to separate us.

I cannot broach
the space between
Shelley and me.
I must find a way
to get my Shelley back.
He wanders
so far from port.

SAILING
Summer 1821

Shelley dreams of the open seas.
He never fears
his ship will meet
rough waters
or too strong a wind.
And if he survives
the mad winds and waves,
he sees his near
misfortune
as a good omen.

I, too, dream of drifting
away with my love,
but we do not board
the same vessel lately.
I do not wish
to raise a full sail
in high wind
and risk disaster.
I want to cruise
about on days
of calm, float
paper boats together
as we did
when we first
fell in love.

BYRON AND SHELLEY

August 1821

Shelley goes to visit Byron alone
as Byron bid him come in a letter.
I surmise
that along the way
he stops to see Claire,
who lives now in Livorno,
supposedly healing from scrofula,
a form of consumption.
She has been prescribed
to bathe in the sea.
This upsets me
like a boat tossed
about by a wicked storm.
I have no recourse
and there is little I can do
but wait it out.

Claire does not know
that Shelley travels to visit Byron,
but believes that Shelley
only stops to check in on Allegra
and her well-being.

Shelley finds the four-and-a-half-year-old
spritely, treated kindly
by all of the nuns.

Byron says he has no intention
to leave Allegra indefinitely
in the convent,
which also reassures us,
and should especially
comfort Claire.

Byron remains in Ravenna
for the time being
though he has said
he wants to follow
his mistress, Teresa,
and her brother and father
out of town.
When Shelley arrives
in Ravenna, Byron tells
him of the terrible gossip
that the Hoppners have spread
like manure about us.
Elise, our former nursemaid,
alleges that Claire is Shelley's mistress
and that the baby born in Naples
and left with foster parents
is the daughter of Shelley and Claire.
Further, the Hoppners claim
that Shelley tried to get
an abortion for Claire
and when that failed
Shelley tried to have the baby adopted.

Shelley begs me to write to Byron
to clear up these matters.
How could anyone suppose that Shelley
would abandon his own child?

I cry tears to fill an urn.
My face stains with sadness.
Then I take out my quill
and refute point by point
everything that Elise
and the Hoppners said.

DOUBT
August 1821

When the winds
of a great storm
bend down trees
and uproot my garden,
I wonder if I shall
cower or stand
amidst the ferocity.

When my child,
hot with fever
and cold with tears,
calls out for aid
I wonder if I shall
hinder or help
him to recover.

When my husband
requests that I refute
rumors that
he has been unfaithful,
I wonder if
my pen lies
or tells truth.

A LETTER FROM MY SHELLEY

Late Summer 1821

My Shelley writes
with a bit of good news,
much needed relief
amidst this landscape of disarray.
He convinces
Byron to come to Pisa
with Teresa. I delight
because Claire shall
certainly want to keep
distance between herself
and the man she so loathes
for sending her daughter
to the convent.

Lastly, Shelley suggests
that Byron and Leigh Hunt
begin a new journal called
the *Liberal*. The Hunts
will now join us in Pisa as well,
and stay with Lord Byron.
My heart expands
like a purse full of pounds.
I will see my dear friends again.

JUGGLING MISTRESSES
Autumn 1821

Byron does not come
directly to Pisa, but remains
in Ravenna for two months.
His mistress, Teresa,
arrives straightaway
and I am the one
who is to visit her
and make her feel
welcome as the wind
on a stifling summer day
here in Pisa.

Claire is also in Pisa.
Happily we are
getting along like
rhythm and drum,
as Shelley and I
entreated Byron to allow Claire
to see her daughter.

Even though we failed
to be granted permission for Claire,
Claire in a mature manner
shows gratitude.
She has been a dear
helping me with little Percy.
The only trouble is
that I must also
attend like a handmaid
to Teresa, Byron's latest mistress.

Claire kindly assists me in choosing
furniture for our new home
on the Lung'Arno,
and for Byron's palazzo
across the river.
She never complains
that she does work
for one she so dislikes,
but cloaks her despair
as though it were
a hideous scar.

Teresa worries that Byron
may never arrive,
as I often did with Shelley.
But come November
Byron shows up in grand fashion
complete with a traveling carriage,
mountains of baggage,
dozens of horses,
and a menagerie of exotic animals.

Claire leaves Pisa
on the day that Byron arrives.
She sees his traveling train
on the road and swears
on her daughter's life,
it will be the last time
they cross paths.

GATHERING A GROUP
OF LIKE-MINDED MALE
INDIVIDUALS
Winter 1821–1822

Shelley believes
we can put down
permanent roots in Italy now;
for like ripples in a pond,
a group of expatriates
gathers to form his
community of friends.
With the Williamses,
the Hunts, and Byron
we will be assured good company.

Byron centers the group.
He lives at the Palazzo Lanfranchi,
a cavernous Renaissance building
overlooking the Arno
that frightens his servants
with its creaks and moans
and is said to be haunted by ghosts.

When Edward Williams
meets Byron, the celebrity,
he awes over his grandeur
as one is astounded
by a great blue whale.

Shelley's cousin, Thomas Medwin,
also arrives to join our group.
Medwin decides he will record
all of Lord Byron's words
and thoughts. We tease him
for his incessant scribbling,
and Byron says more
and more fanciful things
to aid Thomas's pen.

Byron arranges a schedule
based upon his preference
for rising late. The men—
Shelley, Pietro Gamba (Teresa's brother),
Medwin, John Taafe, and Edward—
ride out to a farm
to have shooting contests.
All the horses and arrangements
are courtesy of Byron.
Sometimes we ladies
attend the shooting match,
but often I stay back
at the house to care
for Percy and read and write.

Byron generally dines alone
and then calls upon Teresa
as though she were a servant.
Every Wednesday Byron hosts
dinner parties for his new
acquaintances, but these
are male affairs, with heavy
eating and drinking.

Shelley and Edward
lounge around Byron's palazzo
on days when rain
makes walking unviable,
and they play billiards.

Shelley produces not
as much work as he would like,
but I think, as one overwhelmed
by a hurricane,
the immense productivity
and character of LB
humbles and intimidates him.

I reduce to picking
flowers and talking morality
with Jane. But I miss being part
of the political and poetical
conversations of the men.

MY FATHER'S PRAISE

Winter 1822

When I sink low or need
a little inspiration for my writing
I remember the words
my father bestowed
upon my first novel,
"the most wonderful work
to have been written
at twenty years of age
that [he] has ever heard of."
His praise buoys me
through deep and rough tides.
I regain energy to swim to shore.

MORE SEPARATION
Winter 1822

Though it chills not outside,
inside our apartments
it often feels icy.
Shelley and I, unlike
Jane and Edward, do not steal
off to find moments alone lately.
We grow like two trees
whose limbs and roots
may be intertwined
but who nevertheless stem
upwardly apart.

Edward Trelawny now
arrives in Pisa. He claims
to know everything relating
to ships, and Edward Williams
and my Shelley set their hearts
on building a boat.
Trelawny, of course,
knows the perfect man
to craft them one.

Trelawny is like sugar
mixed with butter.
Because of his brooding figure
and tales of fantastical adventure,
I enjoy him immediately
as does everyone in our circle.

Jane and I question
Shelley and Edward's
designs to construct a boat,
but boys will be boys
and we have little to say about it.

I enter more into Pisan
society, attending balls
and the sort of functions
that bring repulsion to my lover's eyes.
He refuses my idea to host a party.

I send my novel *Valperga*
to my father for publication
after Shelley's editor
refused to look at it.
It pains me that we are
no longer united
even in our literary accomplishments,
very different from when
we worked together
on *Frankenstein*.

I copy Byron's poems for him
and recopy the cantos of *Don Juan*
into a more readable form.
I amuse my toddler Percy
and prepare for the arrival
of the Hunts. I bake mince
pies for a Christmas
that I do not spend
with Shelley as all the men
celebrate it together at Byron's.

I do all of these things alone,
like a duet of only one voice,
without the one I most love.

DANCING AT A BALL
Winter 1822

My feet glide
across the floor
and I am swept up
in a moment of ardor
and light
like one sprinkled
with fairy dust.

I forget
worry and woe
and embrace
movement.
Twirls of happiness
kiss my forehead,
and I fly free.

My only wish
is that my Shelley
was here to partner me.

JANE WILLIAMS

Winter 1822

Shelley's new infatuation
appears to be Jane.
He admires her easy
way and her singing voice
and buys her a guitar.
I believe he may
write secret poems
to her as he did
with Claire in the past.

I know this is just
Shelley's way of the sun
and expect that the infatuation
will pass, but sometimes it makes
me feel as though
I am a garment of clothing
with holes and stains
no longer wearable.
Shelley is not one to be material
in his possessiveness,
but pretty new things
often attract his attention.

I try to speak to Edward
about this but he seems
a little flattered
that Shelley takes
an eye to Jane.
I try to remember
that this too shall pass,
although has it ever really
passed with Claire?

At least I become pregnant
again, so old clothing
or not I am not completely
disposable.

A CATASTROPHE
March 24, 1822

On the way home from shooting,
Shelley, Byron, Pietro, Trelawny,
Taafe, and Captain Hay
meet an Italian dragoon called Masi.
Teresa and I watch the action
from a nearby carriage.

Masi gallops toward Taafe
and knocks him from his horse.
Then my Shelley chases Masi,
and a confrontation arises
wherein Shelley's face is cut
by Masi's sword,
and Shelley and Captain Hay
are thrown from their horses
like there has been a joust.

Masi then disappears
back into the city,
cowardly among the crowds.

Byron and his servants find him,
and Byron challenges Masi
to a duel, but as a throng gathers
one of Byron's servants
stabs Masi in the stomach
with a pitchfork.
Masi is expected to die.

Much fuss occurs
over these events because
it will be murder if Masi dies.

Thankfully he lives.
I record everyone's account
of the incident for the police
at Byron's request.

We are now as notorious
in Pisa as we are in England.
They banish Byron's servant
from the city.

We can go nowhere
without scandal it seems.

I tell Byron I prefer
when he sends me his
poems to copy out.

MY FAIR HAND
Spring 1822

I transcribe the brilliant lines
of Byron and Shelley
in my fair hand.

I trace family lines
of writers and philosophers
on my fair hand.

I nurture a small child
in body and spirit
with my fair hands.

But sometimes I wonder,
when the wind throws
whirlwinds round my feet,
if I *have* a fair hand?

ALLEGRA
Spring 1822

Before Byron left Ravenna
the mother superior of the convent
invited him to visit his daughter Allegra.
Allegra wrote to ask her father to come and see her.
He neither answered his daughter's letter,
nor dropped by the convent.

In February 1822,
Claire planned to take
a job as a governess in Vienna.
She begged Byron to allow her
to see Allegra before she left.
Byron refused, so Claire
remained in Florence
instead of going to Vienna.

By the early spring,
Claire hatches a scheme
wherein we should liberate
Allegra from her cage
of the convent.
Shelley and I stand
firmly against this
as it is as foolish
as going shoeless in the snow.
Byron will certainly find out,
and with his money and power
could destroy us all.
He might even engage Shelley
in a duel over his daughter.

Claire gives up her crazy
ideas of freeing Allegra,
but fears that her daughter ails.

In April, we find out
that Allegra has died from typhus.
She is only five years old.
Teresa breaks the news
to Byron, who at first
is devastated and cannot
be moved from his chair,
but then never wishes
Allegra's name to be mentioned
to him again.

I fear Claire's reaction.
She overhears us discuss
the convent and guesses
that something is wrong with Allegra.
On April 30 we inform her
that her dear daughter has died.
Shelley worries Claire will
go mad from grief,
but she remains solid
as an iceberg. Of course,
we cannot see
all that floats beneath
the surface.

SYMPATHY

Spring 1822

We share more than
the loss of a childhood home now,
Claire and me.

We both know
that sorrow cannot be measured
by the size of a little one's shoe.

A part of you
buries under the earth
never to be retrieved,
a sound without an echo.

I hold my sister's hand,
wordless,
but our grasp understands.

THE RETURN OF CLAIRE
May 1822

Claire comes to Pisa
unannounced on May 21.
She becomes another
member of our group
of exiles, though
she refuses to visit Byron.
She has become calmer
than I have seen her in years,
as though in some ways
the finality of Allegra's death
removes her from the purgatory
in which she suffered.

Shelley and Edward's boat
arrives mid-May and they
delight in
everything about the *Don Juan*
except its name.
Shelley calls it *Ariel*.

I suffer from this pregnancy.
I fear trauma.
Claire allows me some relief
and helps with Percy.
Yet the only time I am truly
happy and feel well
is when aboard the boat *Ariel*.
I lie down with my head
on Shelley's knee.
There I can close my eyes
and allow the wind
and the swift motion
of the boat alone
to soothe me.

I am not sure that
I could handle
even a thimble's worth
of grief right now.

MISCARRIAGE
June 16, 1822

I bleed as though
I have been gutted
and slip in and out
of consciousness.
Jane and Claire
send for a doctor
and ice to slow
the incessant bleeding.

The ice arrives before
the doctor. No one
will say it aloud,
but I have lost so much blood
we all fear that I am going to die,
as my mother did with me.
Shelley forces me
into an ice bath
which stems the flow of blood
until the doctor arrives.
The doctor swears
Shelley saved my life.

For days I can do little more
than crawl from my bed
to the balcony I am so weak.
My dream of a new family
is dead.

There was a kicking,
a beat inside my self,
yet beyond me,
a voice that was squelched out.
And I ask only, why?

THE HARD DAYS
June 1822

I know there are times
when I must be difficult
to bear, when sorrow
strips away my smile
and remorse cripples my limbs.

I know I can be cold
and distant as the moon,
dependent upon and awaiting
light from another.

I close myself off
like an eyelid,
protect myself from
viewing certain horrors,
but obscure myself
from witnessing joy as well.

Still I struggle like a tree
in a tornado
to be good and rooted
for those
who love me most.

THE HUNTS' ARRIVAL
June-July 1822

The Hunts and their six children
finally land in Italy at Genoa
on the twentieth of June.
Shelley rejoices
that they are finally here,
and he and Edward
make plans to sail
to meet them in Genoa.
Marianne Hunt is very ill,
but so too am I,
and I entreat Shelley
please not to go.
But my pleas
are as cries to the deaf,
seen but not heard.

The Hunts change their plans
and decide they will go to Livorno,
so Shelley, Edward, Captain Roberts,
and Charles Vivian, their
one-boy crew,
will sail to meet them there.
I again beg Shelley not to go,
but he refuses me
as though I am but a nagging fly
in this oppressive summer heat.

Before he leaves,
Shelley promises me he will
look for new lodging for us
at Pugnano for the rest of the summer.
This calms me a little
like a handkerchief
offered to the mourning.
Still I have a mind to pack up
Percy and head to Pisa myself.

NO GOOD NEWS FOR MARY
July 1822

On July fourth a most upsetting
letter arrives from Shelley
that he will not in fact
look for a new house at Pugnano
and he cannot say when he will return.
He wishes that I stay in Lerici
where I am in such agony
under the scorching sun
and without him.

He tells me he and Hunt
had a joyous reunion
in Livorno after not seeing
each other for four years.

They then traveled to Pisa,
where the Hunts were installed
in the apartments set aside
for them in Byron's palazzo.
Marianne is said to be in grave
health and all are concerned
for her; the travel has made
her so very weak.
I understand how she feels.

Also the Hunts
are destitute and fully dependent
on the idea of living off the profits
from this new journal Hunt
is to edit with Byron.
Byron tires of the idea
of the journal
before it is even begun.
Byron contemplates leaving
Tuscany altogether, because
Teresa and her family
face trouble here
after the whole Masi affair.

Shelley mends the broken
bond over the journal,
like a tailor stitching up
a tattered suit,
and Byron agrees to stay in Pisa.
But my Shelley maneuvers
much negotiation on Hunt's behalf.

Edward wishes to return to Jane
here in Lerici, as would be
expected of a husband.
I send the saddest of letters
to my Shelley in his absence.
Shelley writes letters to Jane
worried about how she handles
her solitary and melancholy,
but he directs
no sympathy to me.

THEN
July 1822

I lie back against
my mother's gravestone,
and Shelley runs
his fingers through
my fine red hair.
The limbs of the willow
embrace us
with their verdant arms.

His wild eyes
blaze with a passion
I have never known
like a thousand
acres aflame.
I want to say something,
but Shelley
seals my lips.
"All words fail
this moment,"
he says.
I fervently nod my head.

I hear a small whimper
like the wind's whistling cry.
"Mama."
I push the covers
from my bed.
I was reveling
in a lovely dream.

THE STORM

July 8, 1822

The *Ariel* sets sail from Livorno
to come back to Lerici.
The only people aboard
are Shelley, Williams,
and the crew boy, Charles Vivian.
Captain Roberts sees
the boat take leave
and watches some ominous clouds
form on the horizon.
After an hour,
through his telescope Roberts
views a storm come up
and swears he saw the boat
take down its topsails.
But I'm not sure,
for without a deck
and with sails hard to bring down,
even a small but sudden
gust of wind could upset the *Ariel*.
And my Shelley cannot swim.

THE MEN HAVE NOT
RETURNED
July 11, 1822

Claire, Jane, and I
grow more anxious
than mothers of ailing infants.
A letter arrives
from Hunt confirming
that the *Ariel* left Livorno in a storm.
Leigh Hunt wants news
of the travelers' safe arrival.
The suspense is as dreadful
as a nest of vicious cobras.
Jane fears the worst.

Even though I have not left
the villa for nearly a month,
and look more like
a ghost than a woman,
Jane and I depart for Pisa
immediately
and head to Byron's.

Byron provides no news
except that Edward, Shelley,
and Charles Vivian had sailed
the previous Monday in a storm.
We cannot stop to rest,
but take a carriage to Livorno
in search of Trelawny and Captain Roberts.
Roberts tries to assure us
that he saw the topsails
being taken down, though
it must have been hard
to view anything for certain
in the haze of the storm.

Trelawny escorts us back to Lerici.
I feel as though
I shall go into convulsions.
As we cross the river
I fear I plod through
my lover's grave.

Trelawny goes searching
for the men
and when we hear nothing
I gain a bit of hope.

No hope
only death,
as the sad news
finally reaches us
that three bodies
have been discovered.
Trelawny identified Shelley
by the volume
of Keats's poems
found on his person.

SHELLEY'S CALL
August 1822

I can faintly hear
my lover's long-ago call
to join him
so that we shall never
be separated,
but united in death.

No laudanum
can bring back
my Shelley
and I cannot abandon
my child.
I close off
like a coffin lid has slid
over my senses.

Everyone sings praises of Shelley.
I find a bit of comfort in this.
I write to my father that
I feel my Shelley is ever with me.
I must live to be good and wise,
then I will deserve to join
Shelley someday.

A FUNERAL
August 16, 1822

As I paralyze in grief,
Trelawny arranges the funeral.
Williams and Shelley
will be exhumed from
the graves on the beach
where they were found,
and they will be burned to ash.

As my father could not bear
to attend my mother's funeral,
I cannot be present at my love's burial.
I stay at home and write
a letter to Maria Gisborne.
I lament the fact that
Shelley and I were fighting
on the day he left
and that I begged him to stay.
I feel guilt and sorrow.
I miss my love
more than I can express.
Thank goodness for my little
Percy.

Shelley's friends built a portable
structure on which to burn the bodies
and brought frankincense,
salt, wine, and oil to sprinkle
on the men.

Trelawny said that
the scenery on the shore
was as lonely and grand
as Shelley's poetry.
He and Byron and Hunt
imagined that Shelley's spirit
soared above them.
Byron swam out to his boat,
the *Bolivar*, while Leigh Hunt
remained in the carriage
and Trelawny watched
Shelley's body burn for four hours.

The flames were incandescent
as was Shelley, and they consumed
all of him, except his heart.

I keep Shelley's heart
close to me always,
preserved in wine and stored
in my portable writing desk.
Whenever I need
inspiration or stimulus
my dear love's remains
will remind me
that I now have not only
my parents' legacy to consider
but also my Shelley's.
I must keep alight his flame.

ELEGY FOR MY SHELLEY
1822

We built a world of words
and yet none satisfy now.

If you are ash
where do I store my heart?

If you are buried
who will teach our child
to say "yes"
in a foreign tongue?

If you are spirit
who will craft poems
that awaken the soul?

If you are memory
what lighthouse
calls your ship to shore?

I vow to lay down my life
to make your name known.

AUTHOR'S NOTE

"Beware; for I am fearless and therefore powerful."
—Mary Shelley, from *Frankenstein*

I love *Frankenstein* because of its gothic origins, its human values, its indelible characters, and its enduring heart. Many things compel an author to write a book, but in the case of *Hideous Love*, what most drew me to the subject matter was Mary's youth and indomitable spirit. A woman of intellect, highly respected now as one of the important writers of her time, Mary broke the mold. She wrote a masterpiece of the English language in her teens. Her life challenged her with its tragedies and strife, and yet, fearlessly, she never gave up. When she left home and traveled with Shelley, a chest of her early writings was lost. This book was inspired in part by the idea that other tales of Mary's adventures were lost along her tangled path.

After the tragic loss of Shelley, Mary spent much of her life compiling his work. In 1839, when his father finally lifted his prohibition against publishing Shelley's writings, Mary brought out an annotated collection of her husband's poetry. Her work helped to establish Percy Bysshe Shelley as one of the greatest poets of his period and of English literature in general. Mary never again married but devoted her life to writing, to raising her son, Percy, and to the promotion of Shelley's work. She also continued to support her father financially. Mary died from a brain tumor in 1851 at the age of fifty-three.

Without question Mary's most iconic and popular work, both during her lifetime and after her death, has been *Frankenstein*. The most universally read version is the 1831 edition of the novel, which Mary revised and to which she added her own introduction, though among scholars there has been some resurgence in reading the original 1818 text. Despite mixed and, sometimes, less than laudatory reviews, *Frankenstein* was a bestseller of its day. The book was even turned into a stage play during Mary's life—the equivalent of becoming a movie today. *Frankenstein* throughout its history has been published in hundreds of editions and is often required reading in high schools and colleges.

I believe this book endures not only because of its multiple themes, its lyrical writing, its feminist principles, and its science fiction origins, but also because it creates universal and intricate characters and situations. The book causes the reader to think with gravity about the nature of life. It also bridges an important place in literary history—the transition from gothic eighteenth-century literature into the realism championed by novels of the nineteenth century. Now nearly two hundred years old, *Frankenstein* still pervades our culture, from movies to postage stamps to cereal boxes to Halloween costumes. Say "Frankenstein" to a young child and the vision of a monster comes to mind, just as it did for Mary that dark and rainy summer night in 1816. Mary Wollstonecraft Shelley and her monster of a book fearlessly pioneered a new type of novel, one that powerfully withstands the test of time.

CAST OF CHARACTERS

(in order of appearance)

MARY WOLLSTONECRAFT GODWIN SHELLEY is best known as the author of *Frankenstein* and as the wife of Percy Bysshe Shelley.

MARY WOLLSTONECRAFT GODWIN is the mother of Mary Shelley and Fanny Imlay. She was a political philosopher of the late 1700s. Often considered the first feminist, she authored the book *A Vindication of the Rights of Woman*. She died eleven days after she gave birth to Mary.

WILLIAM GODWIN is Mary's father and the father of William Godwin Jr. He made his name with his philosophical work *Enquiry Concerning Political Justice*, but wrote and published in many other formats as well, including fiction.

MARY JANE CLAIRMONT becomes Mary's stepmother when Mary is four. She is the mother of Charles Clairmont, Clara Jane Clairmont, and William Godwin Jr.

FANNY IMLAY GODWIN is Mary's older half-sister. They have the same mother, and after their mother's death William Godwin raises Fanny as though she is his daughter and gives Fanny his last name.

CHARLES CLAIRMONT is Mary's older stepbrother. Mary Jane Clairmont is Charles's mother.

CLARA JANE CLAIRMONT (FIRST KNOWN AS JANE, BUT LATER KNOWN AS CLAIRE CLAIRMONT) is Mary's stepsister. Only a few months younger than Mary, Claire plays a crucial role in Mary's love life.

WILLIAM GODWIN JR. is Mary's younger half-brother. William Godwin is his father and Mary Jane Clairmont is his mother.

ISABELLA BAXTER is one of Mary's dearest childhood friends. Mary lives with her family when she is sent to Dundee, Scotland, at fourteen. Mary also becomes close with Isabella's sister, Christina. Isabella Baxter marries David Booth.

PERCY BYSSHE SHELLEY (SHELLEY) eventually becomes Mary's husband. He comes from an aristocratic background, but shuns his heritage. Shelley is renowned as one of the great Romantic poets of the early nineteenth century, though his name was made primarily after his death and largely thanks to the efforts of Mary. He is considered to this day to be one of the best lyric poets in the English language.

HARRIET WESTBROOK SHELLEY is Shelley's first wife and the mother of his two children Ianthe and Charles. Shelley leaves Harriet for Mary, although the marriage is in disrepair even before Shelley meets Mary.

LORD BYRON (GEORGE GORDON BYRON), the first international celebrity, was well known in his day for his poetry, beauty, and rakishness. Byron is still regarded as one of the most influential poets of the Romantic period and one of the greatest British writers.

THOMAS LOVE PEACOCK is a close friend of Percy Shelley's and a writer of poems and satirical novels. Thomas knows Shelley before he begins his relationship with Mary. Peacock becomes Shelley's agent and business adviser.

ELIZABETH AND HELEN SHELLEY are two of Percy's sisters whom he wishes to liberate from boarding school. Beginning with his sisters, Shelley always surrounded himself with a commune of women.

THOMAS JEFFERSON HOGG, a lifelong friend of Shelley's since they met at Oxford, trains to become a barrister. He re-enters Shelley's life in the autumn of

1814 to join Mary, Shelley, and Claire in forming an association of philosophical people. Thomas develops feelings for Mary that she does not return in measure. Hogg writes a biography of Shelley after his death.

SIR TIMOTHY SHELLEY is Percy Bysshe Shelley's father. He lives the life of a country squire and serves in Parliament. He and his son are somewhat estranged. He does not approve of his son's literary aspirations or his lifestyle.

WILLIAM SHELLEY, born January 24, 1816, is Mary and Shelley's first son. His nickname is Willmouse.

JOHN POLIDORI is Lord Byron's traveling doctor on his trip to Geneva, as well as his biographer. Polidori takes a liking to Mary and participates in the ghost-story-writing contest that spawns *Frankenstein*. John eventually writes a story about a vampire that establishes the modern conception of what constitutes a vampire. He commits suicide at age twenty-five.

AUGUSTA BYRON is Lord Byron's half-sister, with whom he is rumored to be in love. This relationship destroys his first marriage. The affair causes such scandal that Byron leaves England.

LEIGH HUNT is an English critic, essayist, poet, and writer. He edits *The Examiner*, a periodical whose politics landed him and his brother John in prison for libel against the reigning prince regent. He gathers a circle of literary, philosophical, musical, and political people around him, including Shelley, Mary, and Lord Byron.

ELIZA WESTBROOK is the sister of Shelley's first wife, Harriet. She fights for custody of Shelley's first two children but is denied custody, as is Shelley.

IANTHE AND CHARLES SHELLEY are the two children that Harriet and Shelley have together. When Shelley loses custody of Ianthe and Charles, he never again visits them.

CLARE ALLEGRA BYRON (ALLEGRA) is the offspring of Lord Byron and Claire. Allegra is Claire's only child.

MARIANNE HUNT is Leigh Hunt's wife. She bears him six children.

POLLY ROSE is a Marlow village girl whom Shelley tutors when he lives at Albion House. She is a prime example of Shelley's practice of philanthropy throughout his life.

CLARA EVERINA SHELLEY is Mary and Shelley's third child and their first girl to live long enough to be given a name.

ELISE DUVILLARD FOGGI is the devoted nursemaid of the Shelleys. They send her to Byron's to help care for Allegra. She later marries Shelley's manservant Paolo Foggi.

MARIA GISBORNE cares for Mary and Fanny when they are young children after the death of their mother. When Mary meets Maria again, she is living in the Italian town of Livorno, where Mary and Shelley take up residence for a period.

HENRY REVELEY is the grown-up son of Maria Gisborne who grows attached to Claire and proposes to her.

RICHARD HOPPNER is the Venetian British consul who, along with his wife, takes care of Allegra for a time.

PAOLO FOGGI is Shelley's manservant and a beloved employee of the family until he later impregnates Elise Duvillard and is forced to leave their employment. He later blackmails Shelley over the baby of Naples.

ELENA ADELAIDE SHELLEY is "the baby of Naples." Her parentage remains a mystery to this day, although it is certain that Mary, although registered as such, is not her mother.

AMELIA CURRAN is an artist who paints a portrait of William Shelley and who lives in Rome at the same time as Mary and Shelley. She also paints the only surviving portrait of Claire, which Claire is said to have detested.

PERCY FLORENCE SHELLEY is Mary and Shelley's fourth child, and their only child who will reach adulthood.

TERESA GUICCIOLI is Lord Byron's mistress. He lives with her family as her acknowledged escort even though she is still married to her husband.

THOMAS MEDWIN is Shelley's cousin who introduces Shelley and Mary to the Williamses. Thomas writes an account of the time he spends with Byron when the great Lord Byron lives in Pisa.

EDWARD WILLIAMS is an Englishman who, along with his wife, Jane, becomes a part of the Shelleys' Pisan circle. He and Shelley build the sailboat the *Ariel* together.

JANE WILLIAMS is Edward Williams's unofficial wife. They have two children together. She also catches the eye of Shelley.

EDWARD TRELAWNY joins the Pisan circle of expatriates. He is a storyteller and proclaims to know everything about boats. He finds the man who builds Shelley and Edward Williams their boat, the *Ariel*. Trelawny later writes a controversial memoir of his time with Shelley.

A TIME LINE OF BOOKS
BY MARY SHELLEY

Mounseer Nongtongpaw or The Discoveries of John Bull in a Trip to Paris. London: Printed for the Proprietors of the Juvenile Library, 1808.

In 1808 a thirty-nine-quatrain reworking of Charles Dibdin's five-stanza song *Mounseer Nongtongpaw* was published by the Godwin Juvenile Library. This version became so popular that it was republished in 1830 in an edition illustrated by Robert Cruikshank. There remains some debate over whether or not Mary is the actual author of this work or whether a prose rendering of hers influenced a man by the name of John Taylor to compose the poem.

History of a Six Weeks' Tour through a part of France, Switzerland, Germany, and Holland, with Letters descriptive of a Sail round the Lake of Geneva, and of the Glaciers of Chamouni. London: Published by T. Hookham, jun., and C. & J. Ollier, 1817.

Mary based this book (1817), which directly preceded *Frankenstein*, on journal entries and long letters home to Fanny. She used her mother's *Letters Written during a Short Residence in Sweden, Norway, and Denmark* (1796) as a literary model. Mary wrote from an outsider's perspective, though it is a lovely travelogue. She included Shelley's poem "Mont Blanc" in this book.

Frankenstein, or The Modern Prometheus, 3 volumes. London: Lackington, Hughes, Harding, Mavor & Jones, 1818; revised edition, 1 volume, London: Henry Colburn & Richard Bentley, 1831; 2 volumes, Philadelphia: Carey, Lea & Blanchard, 1833.

Nearly two hundred years after it was first published, *Frankenstein* continues to be read as one of the classic novels in the English language and stands as one of the earliest examples of science fiction. Mary began the book in June of 1816 at the age of eighteen and finished the main writing of it by May of 1817. There are numerous interpretations of *Frankenstein*, as is true of all of Mary's writing. One reading of the text supposes the theory that it is a book about the divided self. The idea is that within the civilized man or woman exists a monstrous, destructive force. The creature that emerges from Frankenstein's experiment reflects the loneliness of both the scientist, Victor Frankenstein, and the narrator, Robert Walton. All three characters long for a friend or companion. Frankenstein and his monster alternately pursue and flee from each other. Like fragments of a mind in conflict with itself, they represent polar opposites that are not reconciled and that destroy each other at the end. *Frankenstein* endures because of its abundant philosophical inquiries.

Mathilda, edited by Elizabeth Nitchie. Chapel Hill: University of North Carolina Press, 1959.

After *Frankenstein*, Mary Shelley wrote the novella *Mathilda*, which was never published in her lifetime, partially because her father found it detestable. A rough draft was originally titled *The Fields of Fancy* (after her mother's unfinished tale *Cave of Fancy*, written in 1787). Although not completely autobiographical, the book contains many elements that are self-reflective. For example, the three characters—Mathilda; her father; and Woodville, the poet—represent Mary Shelley, Godwin (Mary's father), and Percy Shelley. The novella is in the form of memoirs addressed to Woodville, composed by a woman who expects to die at twenty-two. Written during the late summer and autumn of 1819, when Mary struggled with depression over the deaths of two children in nine months, *Mathilda* is both furious and elegiac, full of accountability and rife with self-pity. *Mathilda* may be Mary's most famous work next to *Frankenstein*.

Valperga or The Life and Adventures of Castruccio, Prince of Lucca, 3 volumes. London: G. & W. B. Whittaker, 1823.

Mary Shelley began writing her novel *Valperga* in April 1820 in Florence and was still working on it in Pisa that fall. Difficult years elapsed in Mary Shelley's life between the novel's first inception and its completion in the autumn of 1821, which is somewhat indicated by the title change from *Castruccio, Prince of Lucca* to *Valperga*. The focus of the novel, published in 1823, changes from Castruccio's tale to the story of the heroine, Euthanasia. Mary's father helped her edit this book. *Valperga* shares with *Frankenstein* and *Mathilda* the theme of the fall from the innocent, happy illusions of childhood into the reality of adulthood with its knowledge of suffering. *Valperga* was the last book Mary wrote while Shelley was still living.

The Last Man, 3 volumes. London: Henry Colburn, 1826; 2 volumes, Philadelphia: Carey, Lea & Blanchard, 1833.

In February 1824, about a year and a half after Percy's drowning, Mary began to write her bleakest novel, *The Last Man*. *The Last Man* has been called a combination of forms—a work of science fiction, an apocalyptic prophecy, a dystopia, a gothic horror, and a domestic romance. Envisioning a horrifying and disastrous future world, it chronicles the disappearance of the inhabitants of Earth as people are killed by war, emotional conflict, or a mysterious plague. It was Mary's darkest and worst-reviewed book during her lifetime.

The Fortunes of Perkin Warbeck, 3 volumes. London: Henry Colburn & Richard Bentley, 1830; 2 volumes, Philadelphia: Carey, Lea & Blanchard, 1834.

The Fortunes of Perkin Warbeck was perhaps Mary

Shelley's least successful novel. Impressed by the popularity of Sir Walter Scott's historical romances, Mary attempted one based on the historical figure Perkin Warbeck, who claimed to be the younger son of King Edward IV. She was under some constraints in the composition of the novel. Mary created Perkin Warbeck as a stereotypically perfect character and then had to manipulate that character to adhere to historical truths.

Lodore, 3 volumes. London: Richard Bentley, 1835; 1 volume, New York: Wallis & Newell, 1835.

Mary Shelley's novel *Lodore* is semi-autobiographical and repeats the triangle of characters found in *Mathilda*: father-daughter-lover. The most popular and successful of her novels since *Frankenstein*, *Lodore* was the first of Mary's novels to have a sentimental, happy ending.

Lives of the Most Eminent Literary and Scientific Men of Italy, Spain, and Portugal, volumes 86-88 of *The Cabinet of Biography*, in *Lardner's Cabinet Cyclopedia*, conducted by Reverend Dionysius Lardner. London: Printed for Longman, Orme, Brown, Green & Longman and John Taylor, 1835-1837; republished in part as *Lives of the Most Eminent Literary and Scientific Men of Italy*, 2 volumes. Philadelphia: Lea & Blanchard, 1841.

Mary Shelley became increasingly interested in nonfiction as she aged and wrote three volumes in the Reverend Dionysius Lardner's popular *Cabinet Cyclopedia*. He had probably read her essays on Italian literature in the *Westminster Review* and commissioned similar work for his series.

Falkner, 3 volumes. London: Saunders & Otley, 1837; 1 volume, New York: Harper & Brothers, 1837.

In her last novel, *Falkner*, Mary Shelley explored another father-daughter relationship. In this book it is between an orphaned girl and her dastardly Byronic guardian, Falkner. *Falkner* is a perfect finale to Mary's fictional writing as it encapsulates many of her concerns and uses her greatest novelistic strengths: a hero in conflict with himself, an absent mother, love and domestic responsibility, destiny and victimization—elements she had combined in the writing of *Frankenstein* nineteen years earlier.

Lives of the Most Eminent Literary and Scientific Men of France, volumes 102 and 103 of *The Cabinet of Biography*. London: Printed for Longman, Orme, Brown, Green & Longman, 1838, 1839; republished in part as *Lives of the Most Eminent French Writers*, 2 volumes. Philadelphia: Lea & Blanchard, 1840.

At the same time Mary was writing about eminent French writers, she was finally able to compile her husband's work and poetry into four volumes as Sir Timothy (Percy's father) lifted his prohibition of publishing Percy Bysshe Shelley's work. Mary accomplished both enterprises beautifully even though her health began to decline during this period.

Rambles in Germany and Italy in 1840, 1842, and 1843, 2 volumes. London: Edward Moxon, 1844.

Mary's last book, an account of summer tours on the Continent with her son Percy Florence and his college friends, was published in 1844. By then she was in ill health, and in 1848 she began to suffer what were, apparently, the first symptoms of the brain tumor that eventually took her life.

Posthumous Works

The Choice—A Poem on Shelley's Death, edited by H. Buxton Forman. London: Printed for the editor for private distribution, 1876.

Tales and Stories, edited by Richard Garnett. London: William Paterson, 1891.

Proserpine & Midas: Two Unpublished Mythological Dramas, edited by A. Koszul. London: Humphrey Milford, 1922.

Mary Shelley's Journal, edited by Frederick L. Jones. Norman: University of Oklahoma Press, 1947.

Mathilda, edited by Elizabeth Nitchie. Chapel Hill: University of North Carolina Press, 1959.

Collected Tales and Stories, edited by Charles E. Robinson. Baltimore & London: Johns Hopkins University Press, 1976.

The Journals of Mary Shelley, 2 volumes, edited by Paula Feldman and Diana Scott-Kilvert. Oxford: Clarendon Press, 1987.

SUGGESTED FURTHER READING

(and partial sources list)

Bennett, Betty, ed. *The Letters of Mary Wollstonecraft Shelley*, 3 volumes. Baltimore: Johns Hopkins University Press, 1980, 1983, 1988.

Feldman, Paula, and Diana Scott-Kilvert, eds. *The Journals of Mary Shelley*, 2 volumes. Oxford: Clarendon Press, 1987.

Fraistat, Neil, and Donald H. Reiman, eds. *Shelley's Poetry and Prose: A Norton Critical Edition, Second Edition*. New York: W.W. Norton & Company, 2002.

Hay, Daisy. *Young Romantics: The Tangled Lives of English Poetry's Greatest Generation*. New York: Farrar, Straus and Giroux, 2010.

Holmes, Richard. *Shelley: The Pursuit*. New York: Viking Penguin, Inc., 1974.

Hoobler, Dorothy and Thomas. *The Monsters: Mary Shelley and the Curse of Frankenstein*. New York: Little, Brown and Company, 2006.

McGann, Jerome J., ed. *Lord Byron: The Major Works including Don Juan and Childe Harold's Pilgrimage*. New York: Oxford University Press Inc., 1986.

Robinson, Charles E., ed. *Mary Shelley (with Percy Shelley) The Original Frankenstein*. By Mary Shelley (with Percy Shelley). New York: Random House, Inc., 2009.

Seymour, Miranda. *Mary Shelley*. London: John Murray (Publishers) Ltd., 2000.

www.litgothic.com/Authors/mshelley